PUSH GIRL

PUSH

CHELSIE HILL

THOMAS DUNNE BOOKS
ST. MARTIN'S GRIFFIN ✾ NEW YORK

GIRL

A NOVEL

JESSICA LOVE

THOMAS DUNNE BOOKS.
An imprint of St. Martin's Press.

PUSH GIRL. Copyright © 2014 by Sundance TV LLC. All rights reserved. Printed in the United States of America. For information, address St. Martin's Press, 175 Fifth Avenue, New York, N.Y. 10010.

www.thomasdunnebooks.com
www.stmartins.com

Designed by Anna Gorovoy

The Library of Congress Cataloging-in-Publication Data is available upon request.

ISBN 978-1-250-04591-1 (hardcover)
ISBN 978-1-4668-4605-0 (e-book)

St. Martin's Griffin books may be purchased for educational, business, or promotional use. For information on bulk purchases, please contact Macmillan Corporate and Premium Sales Department at 1-800-221-7945, extension 5442, or write specialmarkets@macmillan.com.

First Edition: June 2014

10 9 8 7 6 5 4 3 2 1

Raising
Spinal Cord
Injury Awareness

I would like to dedicate this book to those who have been affected by drinking and driving, a heartbreak, or are feeling like they have lost the only thing that matters. I want people to know that even if they feel like they have lost the only thing that matters, there is still hope. I hope this book inspires people of all ages to never give up!

—CHELSIE HILL

To my grandmother, Ruth MacDonald, for her un-flinching, unwavering, and unconditional love.

—JESSICA LOVE

ACKNOWLEDGMENTS

Endless thanks to my agent, Jill Corcoran, for your belief in me from Day 1, and to Kat Brzozowski and Brendan Deneen, rock-star editors. Working with you all has been a dream.

To Chelsie Hill, thank you for trusting me with your experiences. It was such a pleasure to work with you on bringing Kara's story to life.

To Elizabeth Briggs and Katy Upperman, my saints and saviors. Your brilliant advice, constant cheerleading, and words of wisdom kept me grounded and going when I needed it most. There aren't enough thank-yous in the world for everything you've done for me, so I hope hugs, cupcakes, and exclamation point–filled e-mails will suffice.

To my Indisputably Awesome girls and my NBC Writers, thank you all for being my support system and my sounding board. Your endless patience for my ridiculous questions and your understanding and encouragement at any time of the day or night are what keeps my head above water and a smile on my face, even when all seems lost.

Finally, to my parents for nurturing my creativity in every form from the second I was born, and to my husband for understanding that I really was doing something productive when I sat on the couch with my laptop for hours on end. Thank you for your support, your encouragement, and your love.

—JESSICA LOVE

push girl \\'push 'gər(-ə)l\\ *noun*

1. A fierce, fearless woman who doesn't let life's challenges get in the way of what she wants.
2. Anyone who overcomes adversity with a never-say-die attitude and sense of humor.

PUSH GIRL

CHAPTER 1

Even a perfect boy was allowed a flaw or two.

At least, that was what I tried to tell myself as I stood outside my dance studio alone, waiting for Curt to pick me up. He wasn't always late, only when he lost track of time at the gym. So I don't even know that I'd call his tardiness a flaw, really. More like a small blemish.

But still, it sucked waving good-bye to all my dance friends and saying, "I'm sure he'll be here soon. You don't have to stick around for me." Especially because I wasn't actually sure when he was going to show up, since I'd spaced and left my phone in his truck when he dropped me off earlier.

But it's not like he'd actually forget about me. He did that only one time, and it was totally an accident.

Craning my neck to get a look at every vehicle that pulled into the parking lot was making me into a crazy person, so I decided to keep myself busy by running through the routine

I'd just spent the past hour rehearsing. It was a lyrical dance for the upcoming fall recital, and the other seniors and I each had pretty significant solos during the middle of it. I started taking myself through the moves, but the dance studio was in a shopping center with a grocery store, a nail salon, and an insurance office. Not exactly the ideal location to break it down in the parking lot. So instead of a full double pirouette as I moved through the routine, I pulled my right foot up to my opposite knee and rose on my left toe, hitting the fingers on my right hand to my left palm twice. A pointed toe hovered just above ground level for a beat to indicate a kick; a small kick with my hands out to either side for a jeté.

My muscles ached to dance full out, to kick as high as I could and leap up into the air, but the sidewalk wasn't the place for a show. If only my class wasn't the last one of the night; actually practicing in the studio would have been a much more productive use of my time.

I'd run through the entire routine four times by the time Curt pulled his lifted truck into the parking lot, honking the whole way.

"Finally," I mumbled, grabbing my bag from the ground and walking toward the passenger side. But I rearranged my face into a smile when I crawled up into his truck.

"Sorry I'm a little late, babe," he said after kissing me on the cheek. "Today was back and shoulders, and you know how I get into those lat pulldowns."

"It's cool." It wasn't cool, but one look at Curt Mitchell's big brown eyes and rock-solid biceps made me forget my irritation over waiting alone almost thirty minutes as the streetlights flickered on. I could never stay mad at him. What could I say? His hotness did strange things to my head.

"You left your phone." He cocked his head toward the center console. "It was beeping at me the whole way over here."

Huh, that wasn't normal. Usually the only person who ever blew up my cell was Curt. However, it wouldn't have surprised me if he had texted me a bunch of times and then wondered what that beepy noise in his truck was. I grabbed my phone from the console and scrolled through my texts.

"So, how was rehearsal?" he asked, turning the volume down on the playlist I'd made for him. "Learn any new moves?"

"Great," I said, not looking up. "The lyrical is really coming together. I need to do some more work on my solo, though." I spared him the specifics, since I was pretty sure he cared about the details of my dancing about as much as I cared about hearing the play-by-play of his lat pulldowns.

"What's so interesting over there?" He jabbed a playful elbow into my shoulder. "You're staring at your phone like it holds all the answers to life's problems. Everything okay?"

The texts waiting for me weren't interesting. They were annoying. My mom, whose only job seemed to be keeping her nose up in my business at all times, wanted me home immediately after I left the studio, but she didn't give a reason. Looked like no post-rehearsal make-out time for me and Curt today, since we were already running late. Thanks for the salt in my game, Mom. Then, one from my kinda-sorta best friend Amanda, and my ex-boyfriend Jack with another one of his ridiculous "fun facts."

1 IN 5,000 NORTH AMERICAN LOBSTERS ARE BORN BLUE. HAPPY FRIDAY!

I rolled my eyes. "Yeah. Everything's fine. Just a bunch of stuff I don't want to deal with." I tossed my phone into my bag and kicked it for good measure. "But I do need to go straight home. Looks like Dance Mom's in a mood again."

Curt shook his head. "What's up with her lately? She's really cracking down on you."

"Oh, it's always something with her and Dad these days. They're fighting like cats and dogs." I stuck my thumbnail into my mouth and chewed on it for a second. "Do your parents do that? Fight?" Curt and I had been a couple for almost a year now—eight months and three weeks, to be exact—and after we got home from hanging out at school, we would text and chat online and talk on the phone almost all night. For some reason, though, I couldn't bring myself to share anything serious with him. I'd try to bring up my parents or things that were bothering me, but I'd always chicken out as soon as the conversation got too real.

He adjusted his rearview mirror. "My parents? The biggest problem they have is that my dad prefers the Chinese food my mom makes, and my mom'd rather just cook hamburgers all the time." Curt's half-Chinese, half-white, all gorgeous, with a magazine-perfect family, which was why I never really brought up my own home troubles with him. He wouldn't get that my parents hadn't said anything nice to or about each other for at least two months now. Maybe three.

He peeked at me from the corner of his eye. "What's bothering you, babe? You know you can talk to me if something's on your mind. That's what I'm here for. I can handle the tough stuff."

"I know." I chewed on the tip of my thumb as I stared out the window. "Forget it. It's not a big deal." I didn't make a habit of lying to my boyfriend; it's just that I was scared that if he saw my ugly side—that I sometimes hated my parents for not keeping their fighting to themselves and I wanted to run away every now and then; that I'd once daydreamed for a good ten minutes about pushing Amber, my closest dance friend and biggest studio rival, off the stage so I could dance our duet as a solo; or even that I sort of hated water polo, the sport he dedicated as much time and passion to as I did to dance—that he'd be done with me like last night's homework. Not that I sat around comparing boyfriends, but because I'd known my ex Jack forever, I'd always been comfortable talking to him about any random thing, silly or serious. With Curt, though, I didn't know.

It was exhausting trying to be the perfect girlfriend all the time, but I didn't want to give him a reason to wake up and realize he should be with someone less of a disaster. I'd hoped that he'd reveal something scandalous about his family life to make me feel better about my situation, but it looked like the constant state of war between my parents really wasn't normal after all.

"Kara." He tried to sound stern, but his voice gave away a hint of playfulness. "I can tell something's up."

"I think my dad is just stressed at work," I mumbled, still looking out the window.

He moved one hand from the steering wheel and rested it high up on my leg. "But the question is," he said, rubbing circles on my thigh with his thumb, "are your parents going to be cool with you coming to Rob Chang's party tonight? Am I going to have to crawl up your trellis and sneak you out? Or are you going to have to throw that long blond hair out the window for me?"

It was a good thing I had tights on under my shorts, or he'd have been able to feel all the goose bumps popping up all over my leg.

"Well, first of all," I said, smiling, "I don't have a trellis. And, no, my parents are not cool with me going to the party. But they are fine with me going to the movies with some friends, which is what I told them I would be doing tonight."

He eased the truck to a stop at a red light and leaned across the center console, nuzzling into my neck. "You sneaky girl," he said into my ear. "I'm such a bad influence on you."

It's true that my world pretty much turned upside down when I started dating Curt. With over four thousand students, Pacific Coastal High School was way too huge to have a "popular crowd." So it's not like I was some outcast plucked from obscurity and thrust into high school stardom when my dancing captivated him at last year's studio fall recital, when he was there watching his little sister. But as soon as the gorgeous water polo captain welcomed me into his life, I found myself invited to parties that I didn't know happened on the weekends and hanging out with people I'd only ever come into contact with when I waited behind them in the bathroom line. It was pretty unbelievable to kick off my senior year with an invitation to Rob Chang's back-to-school party, something Past Kara would only have heard about on Monday morning from the people sitting behind her in English.

"You are absolutely ruining my senior year," I said. Then I giggled. I couldn't help it. He was nibbling on my earlobe. "Go. It's green."

"You know what's really going to ruin your senior year?" He turned into my neighborhood, and part of me wanted to tell him to flip a U-turn and keep driving around so I didn't have to go home yet. But I knew I'd have to face the Wrath of Mom for that choice, so I kept quiet.

"You leaving me for Rob Chang?"

"How about me, Rob, and the rest of the varsity water polo team officially nominating you as our Homecoming Queen candidate?"

"What?" I squealed. "Are you serious? Nominations just opened today. You guys have an entire month to choose someone to represent water polo. What if you change your minds?"

Curt pulled into my driveway, turned off his truck, and shifted in his seat so he was facing me. "Don't be ridiculous, Kara. I'm the captain of the team. You're my girlfriend. Who else would we choose?" He reached his hand up to my face, running his fingers through my hair; then he leaned over the console again, this time kissing me lightly. "Unless you were planning on breaking up with me sometime in the next month or something."

I smiled back at him, this gorgeous, perfect boyfriend of mine. "No way, man," I said. "You're stuck with me."

"How was rehearsal today?" Mom's voice was terse as she banged around in the kitchen, and an obvious tension filled the house. It slammed into me the second I walked through the door. I knew it wasn't me she was upset with, but that didn't matter. When she and Dad fought, it had quite the trickle-down effect.

"Great!" I tried to be as peppy as possible to counteract the tension. "Our lyrical routine for the fall recital is really coming together. Christine used me as an example to the other girls, like, three times, and afterwards she talked to me and Amber about doing a hip-hop duet. You know we've always wanted to do one, so we're going to try to throw something together."

I loved dancing, and it came easily to me, but I worked my butt off at it. I always had. I took as many classes as we could afford and my schedule would allow. I was in the studio on evenings and weekends, choreographing, rehearsing, practicing technique. I helped out in the Small Fry class because I loved seeing the little girls fall in love with dancing the way I did. Seeing them discover that this was their passion, their life, just as I had. And Mom was always there, right beside me. She was a total Dance Mom that way, I think because she never had a passion when she was younger. Now her passion was me.

"Mmmm," Mom said as she wiped down the counter, staring intently at a nonexistent mark on the granite. I got the distinct feeling she wasn't listening to me, and I was tempted to start throwing out a bunch of random stuff, maybe a few of Jack's fun facts, just to see if she'd even notice. But I knew better than to push her when she was like this. If she was zoning out during my rehearsal recap, things must be bad.

The weirdness was dulled somewhat when Logan, our little terrier mutt, bounded in from the TV room. "There's my little baby dog," I said, picking him up and hugging him while he licked my face with abandon. "There's my waggy tail. Mom, was Logan a good boy today?"

"What?" Mom said, still wiping the counter.

I shifted a wiggly Logan to one arm and chewed on the thumb of my free hand, waiting for her to register my question and answer me, but I was met only with the sounds of the towel brushing back and forth across the counter. "Okay, then. I'm going upstairs." I returned a squirmy Logan to the ground and he jumped up on my legs as I rummaged through the pantry for a protein bar. "I'm going to take a quick nap before I head to the movies tonight." I was worn out after a long day of school and rehearsal, and I wanted to be at the top of my game at the party. A little power nap, and I'd be good to go.

"Oh, yeah," she said, seeming to snap out of her thoughts. "What time is Amanda picking you up?"

"I'm meeting her there around eight thirty. The movie starts at nine." I hated bringing Amanda into my lie, but if I said I was going out with unnamed friends, Mom would want phone numbers and fingerprints and mothers' maiden names. "Is that okay?"

"It's fine." She abandoned her counter wiping and lowered herself into one of the chairs at the kitchen table. "Your father should be home by then. He's picking up a pizza for dinner."

"Sounds like a plan." I didn't flinch at the daggers in her voice when she brought up Dad, or how she had recently started calling him "your father." I didn't want her to know that I noticed.

Upstairs, I pushed all thoughts of my parents and their ongoing troubles out of my mind. Instead I took a quick shower, and as I brushed out my long tangle of hair, I wondered what to do about the two texts I'd been ignoring since I left the studio.

Text 1: Amanda Kenyon, my best friend since kindergarten, who was a best friend in title more than practice these days. It wasn't for her lack of trying, though. It was me. I'd made all these new friends since I started dating Curt, and Amanda and I had started drifting apart. It happened to friends all the time, I told myself, and it didn't have to be this huge deal. But she didn't seem to want to let go, and she wasn't really taking my hints.

She'd texted to see what I was up to. *Well, Amanda, I'm going to Rob Chang's back-to-school party, and there's no way I'm asking him if I can bring you. Sorry, but it is what it is.*

It's not like I was embarrassed of her; Amanda was great. We looked about as opposite as possible: me, tiny, pale, and blond with a dancer's body; and her, dark skin, long braids, and tall, like I wished I were. But our shared past made us pretty much personality twins, and I really did have a blast every time we were together. She didn't know any of these people, though, since she spent most of her time lately in the school's video production studio or working at the movie theater at the mall. She'd be bored out of her mind at this party, and I'd end up having to hang out with her the whole time. Honestly, if I were going to babysit on a Friday night, I should at least get paid for it.

Text 2: Jack Matthews, my ex-boyfriend. Jack and I were together from eighth grade to the summer after sophomore year. We'd always liked each other, and there was no big dramatic scene when we broke up. It was totally mutual; I thought we should break up and he agreed. I had my dance stuff, after all, and he got elected to Student Government, so it was a perfect time to pull the "moving in different direc-tions" card. I'd say that Amanda should take a lesson from him in accepting change and moving on, which would have been convenient because the two of them were next-door neighbors and practically besties, but the thing is, recently

Jack had started texting me pretty regularly. There was no real point to his texts—they were mainly fun facts or super-cheesy inspiring quotations. (Yesterday I got YOU MISS 100% OF THE SHOTS YOU DON'T TAKE—WAYNE GRETZKY) But still. I kept telling myself that Jack and I were doing the whole exes-as-friends things really well, and that his silly texts were totally innocent. But, at the same time, I wasn't telling Curt about them, either.

Today, I decided to ignore Jack. Sometimes I replied with a fun fact or quotation of my own or asked how Student Government was going, but I wasn't lying to Mom about wanting to take a nap before I headed out for the night. Rehearsal wore me out today.

Ignoring Amanda wasn't an option, though. I didn't want to have a full-on convo, so I replied with GOING TO A PARTY WITH CURT. After a few seconds of consideration, I added a :-) to the end and hit Send.

I plugged my phone into the charger and flopped down on my bed. Logan jumped up next to me and snuggled up into my armpit. "I'm going to have the best night ever, Little Lo," I said, stroking his fur. "Now, what should I wear?" I tried to start planning my outfit, but I slipped off into my nap before I even had a shirt picked out.

CHAPTER 2

I'd like to say it was the smell of pizza that gently lulled me
from my nap, but that would be a lie. It was the yelling, and
it's more like it shoved me out of bed with cold hands.

"I already told you, go out and get a job if you're so miserable!"

"I never said I was miserable. Stop putting words in
my mouth. I just said I don't know what I'm supposed to do.
I haven't worked for seventeen years."

"Volunteer. Work part-time. Do something. Anything!"

"Well, Kara doesn't need—"

"Don't do something for Kara. Do something for yourself.
I swear, you have no life of your own. You have no identity
anymore. I don't even recognize my wife. What happened to
your personality?"

This was bad. I pulled the pillow over my head to drown
them out, but it didn't matter. It's like they were in my room,

yelling at each other on the edge of my bed. Logan gave a whimper and burrowed his fuzzy butt under my covers.

"I don't know if you noticed, but she hasn't needed you in a long time. She can even drive herself to dance and school now."

"So, you just think I'm completely useless, don't you? It doesn't matter that I keep the house clean and make meals and—"

"Of course I don't think that! You're not even listening—"

Since the pillow wasn't working—nothing could drown out the deluge of swearwords that were flying back and forth like daggers now—I decided to give it up. It was time to get ready for the party, anyway. I blasted my music as loud as I could without making it obvious I was trying to tune them out, and I did my best to ignore it all as I put on my makeup. It was no easy feat, because this had to be the worst fight I'd ever heard my parents have. They usually went out of their way to keep from fighting where I could hear them so clearly; I wondered what had happened to make them just not even give a single eff anymore.

I stared at myself in the mirror, zoning out as I tried to plan my escape from the house. It was going to take some James Bond–level sneaking to grab a piece of pizza from the kitchen and creep out the front door without drawing any attention to myself. I was daydreaming up an elaborate plan that involved using Logan as a distraction when the sound of the front door slamming made me jump. I hurried over to my window right in time to catch sight of my dad's SUV backing out of the driveway and peeling off down the street.

Was he leaving? Or was he *leaving* leaving?

I grabbed my phone and my purse and hurried down the

stairs, where I found Mom, her tiny body crumpled up on the couch like a little kid. She wasn't crying, but I could tell that tears were around the corner. Like she was in that place where one wrong word or look would set her off, and it wouldn't be pretty.

"Mom," I said gently, kneeling in front of her. "What happened?"

"Oh, sweetie." She grabbed my hands and pulled me close to her. She tried to hug me, but with me crouching on the floor, she couldn't really get her arms around my shoulders, so I crawled up next to her on the couch. "I'm sorry you had to hear that."

"What happened?" It was impossible to keep the hint of panic out of my voice.

"Your father went to Uncle Kevin's house." She let out a sigh, and her voice was so small. It sounded like she was giving up on everything.

"Is he . . . ?" I wanted to ask if he was coming back. Or when. Or what was going on between the two of them, what the reason was for the constant fighting. But I didn't even know how to form the words. Sure, my parents had been at each other's throats a lot recently, but everyone's parents fought, right? People fight. It's human nature. But is it human nature to scream the way they did tonight? And to storm out?

"Kara. Sweetie." Mom's small voice wavered now. "I know you've heard me and your father fighting a lot recently. We've been having a lot of problems. We thought we could work them out, but we've had these issues in our marriage for a long time now, and—"

I shook my head and grabbed her hand. "Well, it doesn't sound like it's all that big of a deal. Just—"

"Kara, honey, it's way more than just that." She pulled me in close and hugged me as tightly as she could. She took a deep breath and let it out slowly, and I could feel her arms shaking as they tightened around me. "Sweetie, I think your father and I are going to get a divorce."

My stomach dropped to the floor, and I instantly felt a puking sensation. I pulled away quickly, almost launching both of us off the couch with the force of my recoil. "What? A divorce? No."

Mom shook her head. "I'm sorry, sweetie. It's not like we—"

"No. You can't do this." I stood up and backed away from her, as if I could distance myself from what she was telling me. "I can't believe this. Why can't you just work things out? You guys have been together forever. You can't just get a divorce. That's not how it works." I knew I was rambling, but I couldn't keep the words from tumbling from my mouth. Like, if I kept talking, it would change the reality of what she told me.

"Kara, I know you're upset. Sit down and we'll talk about—"

"No." I said. The pukey feeling hadn't gone away, and it had been joined by a pounding in my head. "I don't want to talk about this, because it's not happening. I don't know what you said to Dad, but just call him and tell him you're sorry. Just apologize and get back to normal and move on."

"It's not that easy, sweetie. People don't get divorced over one fight. We've had issues that have been going on for years now, and—"

"Well, fix them, then!" I didn't mean to scream, it just came out, rough and raw. "You're adults. Adults fix their problems; they don't just give up on them. You don't just quit, Mom. Try harder. That's what you tell me. Try. Harder."

"We would never quit without considering all of our options, sweetie. But there are some things we can't just work through. We have to accept that and move on." Mom stood up and reached out to me, but I swatted her arms away.

"I can't believe you," I said. "You tell me to never give up on things that I want. That I can do anything I set my mind to. But look at you. You're just giving up. You can't even follow the advice you give me. Way to be a role model."

And with that, I grabbed my keys from the basket in the entryway and stomped to the door. "I'm going to the movies," I snapped. "Maybe by the time I get back, you two will have figured out how to deal with your problems like the adults you pretend to be." And I slammed the door on her, exactly like Dad had only ten minutes before.

As I buckled myself into my car, I was suddenly even more thankful that I'd agreed to meet Curt at the party instead of having him pick me up. Ever since I got my license the year before, driving had been my Zen. There was something about being on the road with the windows down that helped me sort through my thoughts and clear my head in a way that nothing besides dance had been able to do.

I backed out of my driveway and took the long way to Rob Chang's house. I needed some time to myself to make sense of this world-shaking news.

My parents. Getting a divorce.

This was the absolute worst thing that could happen to me.

CHAPTER 3

My car was in a ditch.

That's how packed Rob Chang's party was by the time I finally finished my drive and showed up. Every free square inch of curb on Meadowlark Lane was occupied, and so was all the parkable space on the adjacent Nightingale and Hummingbird Lanes. My only choices were to block a fire hydrant or squeeze my newly washed Prius into this small ditch next to the fancy remodel project on the corner. Since lawbreaking wasn't really one of my after-school activities, it looked like the ditch was my only option for tonight.

Now I had mud-caked shoes to add to the list of fantastic things that had happened since I woke up from that nap earlier. Tromping through the sludge in these sky-high heels, my shoe of choice since I'd started dating Curt, was really an exercise in balance that would put some of my dance warm-ups to shame. What did I tell myself? Best night ever? Yeah, not so much. But even though my parents and the D-word had ruined the early evening, at least the nine-o'clock hour was still salvageable. I'd been looking forward to this party all week, and I was determined to have fun. Somehow.

I trudged through the ditch dirt until I made it to actual sidewalk, where I ran my shaking hands down the front of my jeans and took a second to collect myself. *You'll see Curt in just a minute,* I thought. *He'll make you feel better. He'll give you a hug and kiss your forehead and make you forget all about the fact that your parents are getting a divorce.*

Just letting the word pop into my head, even in the context of Curt making me feel better about the awful news, brought me instantly back to the fight and Dad storming out and peeling down the street. I shook my head in an effort to clear it all away, but no amount of shaking could erase their words from my head. The fight played in my mind over and over, like a ringing phone I couldn't answer, and it twisted my stomach into knots.

Breathe, I thought. *Breathing will calm you down.*

Even without double-checking the address, I found Rob's house easily, what with the music and the sounds of the crowd that I could hear from halfway down the cul-de-sac. With that and all the cars everywhere, how on earth had no neighbors complained yet? Maybe this was just a really chill neighborhood.

Any sense of calm I'd managed to grab on to dissolved into thin air the second I let myself in to Rob Chang's house. A wall of thumping dubstep smacked me in the face as soon as I cracked the door. The door knocked something into the side table when I swung it open, and a party cup of beer with cigarettes floating in it tipped over and sloshed onto my heels.

So, it really was going to be that kind of night, huh? Well, at least that beer bath washed off the ditch dirt.

Just find Curt, I told myself. *Just find Curt, and everything will be better.*

"Kara!" Two regulars at these parties, Miranda and Kendall, both clad in tiny denim skirts, were squeezed on the couch between two cute sophomores, and it was quite the spectacle to watch them maneuver out of the low seating arrangement without flashing their goodies to the whole room. "You made it!" they squealed in unison, throwing their arms around me in a tangle of limbs and high-pitched excitement. Kara of three hours ago would have returned the enthusiasm and then some, but this Kara could hardly even fake it.

"Have you guys seen Curt?" Balancing on one foot, I used someone's discarded hoodie to wipe off my shoe as I scanned the front room for signs of my boyfriend.

Miranda pointed through the arched doorway at the other end of the room. "He's playing flip cup through there with the water polo boys. Enter at your own risk. It's quite the battle zone."

"They put down the tarp." Kendall gave me a knowing look, and I managed a smile in return. "Come sit with us after you find him, 'kay?" And then the two of them shoehorned themselves back between their sophomores on the couch.

Crossing the front room, I waved to my friends and the people I knew from school, some of whom were orchestrating a little dance-off, but I moved on quickly before they started conversation. I didn't want to be rude, but I also only wanted to talk to Curt. Once I had a big hug from him, once I talked to him about what was going on, then I could try to act like a normal person again.

"There's my girl!" Curt spotted me the second I walked

through the doorway, and hearing his voice calmed me immediately. I hadn't realized how much stress was coursing through my veins until his presence brought my anxiety down to a manageable level. I crunched my way across the tarp covering the carpet and wrapped my arms tightly around his waist.

"I was getting worried about you," he said, nuzzling his face into my hair as he hugged me. "I was starting to wonder if you had ditched me for bigger and better plans."

"Never." I pulled my head away from his chest and scanned the room, which was filled with water polo guys and swimmers, all crammed around a dining table littered with red party cups. "Tonight was the worst. Can we talk somewhere for a minute? Alone?"

During my drive, I'd thought over and over again about what Curt said in the car on the way home from rehearsal— that he could handle the tough stuff, that was what he was there for. I'd been avoiding the topic of my parents with him because I didn't want to be annoying. But I really needed to talk to someone about this, and Curt was my go-to when it came to talking. It would be uncomfortable, but I knew I needed to take this opportunity and really open up to Curt about what was going on with my parents. I had to trust him to listen, help me feel better, and help me get through this.

"I'm sorry." He kissed my forehead, and I couldn't help but smile at the soft pressure of his lips on my skin. "Can you give me like five minutes? We're about to finish up this round, and then Carlos'll be back from the store. He can cover for me, and I can give you my undivided attention."

I caught the disappointment before it hit me too hard, and I took one of my deep, cleansing breaths to keep it away.

He just needed five minutes and then he would be all mine. I could handle five minutes.

"Promise? I really need to—"

"Here, take this, okay?" He waved his hand at one of the beer-filled cups from the table. "Go grab one of the lounge chairs outside and I'll be right there. I promise."

"I'll see you outside." Standing up on my tiptoes, I kissed him quickly on the nose. I turned and walked toward the kitchen, but as I did, my shoe slipped in a river of beer on the tarp, throwing me off balance.

"Whoa," Curt said, grabbing me before I could fall and steadying me by my elbows. "Careful there, babe. You're going to hurt yourself in those shoes."

"I'm fine, I'm fine." Luckily all the water polo boys were too caught up in setting up the next round of flip cup, so they didn't even notice me almost eat it on the beer-soaked tarp. I straightened myself up again and ran my fingers through my hair.

"I can't let the dancing queen hurt those graceful ankles of hers," Curt said, slapping me on the butt. "Oh, and Kara," he said as I turned to walk away. "Don't forget your beer."

"Oh, yeah. Thanks." I took a cup from him and walked toward the kitchen, pushing my way through the people blocking the way out.

Once I was safely in the kitchen, which was considerably less crowded than the flip cup room, I lifted the red cup of beer to my mouth to take a sip. But one big whiff of the sour, foamy beer made me gag like I'd never gagged before. I couldn't help it. With everything on my mind, the beer smell actually made my anxiety worse, if that was possible. I ditched the cup on the kitchen counter and stuck the edge of my thumb in my mouth instead, chewing on what was left of my thumbnail as I scanned the kitchen for some water or soda.

"Aww, sucking your thumb, little baby?"

I hadn't even realized that I wandered right into Jenny Roy's airspace, but there she was, poking around in Rob's fridge, emitting her usual negativity like the stench of a skunk. She was that girl with the perfectly tanned skin, long, black hair in immaculately tousled beachy waves, and the tiniest shorts this side of the toddler section at Nordstrom. She was also the one girl at school who had randomly decided to hate me once I started dating Curt.

"Shut up, Jenny," I mumbled. I was never in the mood for her antics, but today, of all days, it was more likely she would push buttons I usually kept tightly covered. The last thing I wanted to do was let her see me react. *Keep it together, Kara,* I thought. *Ignore her and get outside.*

"What are you even doing here? Besides being in my way?"

I pushed past Jenny, not even trusting myself to respond to her, and I reached into the fridge to grab a bottle of water. She moved out of my way, thank God, but now she blocked the sliding glass door to the backyard. How could someone smaller than me, which wasn't an easy feat in the first place, take up so much room? I knew it would still be a few minutes before Curt made it outside, so I opted for a detour to the bathroom rather than a patio door showdown.

Rob's house was packed with people from school who were talking, dancing around, making out, as well as a bunch of randoms who didn't look familiar at all. His neighbors? People from Santiago High across town? Strangers at the mall he invited into his home? I had no idea. In between the randoms, though, I did see a lot of people I considered friends. Kayla and Ashley from dance. Garrett, Lara, and Jason, part of the crew Curt and I sat with at lunch every day. I waved and smiled and said hellos to them as I passed, but the greetings felt empty. I wasn't in the mood for mindless chitchat. I just needed to talk to Curt. He was the only one who could make me feel better right now.

Or Amanda.

The thought popped up from somewhere in the very back corner of my mind as I washed my hands in the bathroom. If Amanda were here, she would know exactly what to say. When my grandma died back in fifth grade, Amanda came over to my house and we spent the whole night eating ice cream and watching movies to keep my mind off the emptiness and loss that had moved into my heart. She always knew how to turn my mood around.

Grabbing my phone from my back pocket, I hovered my thumb over her speed dial. I couldn't bring myself to press it, though. I hadn't invited her to this party, because I knew she wouldn't know anyone and she'd just be bored. She didn't like these people, and I was tired of explaining why I hung out with them. Despite the happy face I added to the end of her text, I hadn't wanted her here. I couldn't call her. Not now.

I slipped my phone back in my pocket and let out a long sigh as I left the bathroom and headed back down the hall. A line had formed, and the second person waiting, staring at the pictures on the wall, was Curt.

"Babe," he said, and pulled me into a hug. Beer was strong on his breath, but so was the smell of his cinnamon gum. He wasn't too drunk. Yet. "Check out these pictures of Baby Rob. He really should have taken these down."

I turned to face the wall, but I grabbed Curt's arms and kept them wrapped tightly around me as I scanned the little photo gallery. Picture after picture of Rob, his little sister, Reese, and their mom and dad. The backgrounds of the pictures were all different—the four of them at Disneyland on the Mad Tea Party, riding horses along some beach, cheesing in front of Mount Rushmore. But even though the destinations were all different, the pictures were all pretty much the same: Rob and Reese and their mom and dad. All together. A family.

Curt laughed. "Look at that hair. I guess there's a reason he didn't put these on Facebook, huh?"

"Aww, I like them." I said, elbowing Curt gently in the ribs. "I can't believe his parents took him to Paris." I pointed to a photo in the middle of one of the framed collages that featured a wee Rob riding on his dad's shoulders in front of the Eiffel Tower.

Curt snorted. "That's not Paris," he said. "That's Vegas. And look how little Reese was. Who takes a baby to Las Vegas? That's nuts."

"They like to travel as a family," I said, my voice thick with grief. "That's a good thing." I thought back to the cruise I went on to Mexico with Mom and Dad over the summer, and it hit me that it was probably our last family vacation. Ever. If I'd known that, I wouldn't have spent half the time whining about having no cell on the ship and not being able to text Curt. I missed out on our last opportunity for happy family photos. It was over.

Before I could get too lost in my regret, the bathroom door swung open, and it was Curt's turn. "I have to pee," he said, "so you go grab that lounge chair, okay? I'll be right there."

Fortunately Jenny had moved away from the sliding glass

door, so the path to outside was free and clear. There was definitely an unseasonable autumn chill in the air, so aside from the small group surrounding Rob's fire pit, it was pretty empty outside. I snagged a lounge chair, and, leaning back on the cushion, I stared up at the stars in the night sky and replayed my conversation with Mom over and over again, trying to make sense of the strange and scary direction my life had taken in the past few hours.

After about five minutes, I realized Curt should have been out there by now. I grabbed my phone and texted him. HEY BABY, I'M OUTSIDE. Maybe he didn't see me when he came out, because I was lying down.

Ten minutes later, I started wondering if he was having some bathroom troubles or something. It wasn't really how I wanted to think about my hot boyfriend, but what else could be taking so long? YOU OK IN THERE? I texted.

I didn't want to leave the lounge chair, because this was our meeting spot, and the inside of the house was so crowded, I might never track him down in there. He's the one who said to meet here . . . right? Something must have happened. Maybe he was trying to hide from Jenny Roy. I could understand that. I would've been, too.

Fifteen minutes later.

WHERE R U?

After twenty minutes, I broke down and called him. No answer.

At that point I had imagined every terrible thing that could have happened to him between the bathroom and the yard. He'd seen how upset I was, right? He'd told me to wait out here. Why didn't he come?

I jumped up from the lounge chair and paced circles around it. Now my panic over my parents was compounded with a Curt-fueled freakout.

A trip back through the ginormous house to where I'd started told me what I needed to know. Because there was Curt, just like when I first walked in, flip-cupping away as if I wasn't having a total emotional breakdown, alone, on a chaise longue. Well, he was *almost* just like when I first walked in. Two important things had changed.

One, he was now obviously more drunk than he'd been when I left him at the bathroom; his voice was louder, his movements were more exaggerated, like he was putting on a show, and most of the beer from one of the party cups was dribbling down the front of his shirt.

And, two, Jenny Roy now had her arms clasped snugly around his waist.

CHAPTER 4

Jenny Roy was not your typical Mean Girl. I mean, she wasn't at all one of those awful chicks who pushed freshmen into lockers and made catty comments about every girl behind her back. People actually seemed to like her, for the most part. But for some reason I was on her bad side, and her bad side was pretty freaking bad. Word was that she had liked Curt since the dawn of time, and she took it as some sort of personal insult when I started dating him. She'd been pretty awful to me ever since, and I'd been trying to just ignore her because I didn't have time for that nonsense.

But this. This was way too much.

"Curt." I wasn't trying to be loud or cause a scene, but my inside voice wasn't very effective at catching his attention. "Curt!" My voice grew louder now, but it didn't get Curt to look over. Just Jenny.

She tugged on his sleeve, but she stared at me the entire time. "Curt. Someone's looking for you."

"What?" He looked down at her like he only just realized that she had boa-constricted herself around him, and he shook her free. "What'd you say?"

She didn't seem bothered by the fact that she was just shooed off like a fly. "Nothing."

I walked over to him now, since he seemed determined to ignore me. "Curt," I said as I got closer. "What are you doing?" I tried not to sound like the overreacting Overly Attached Girlfriend, but keeping the hurt out of my voice was an impossible task. "You said you were going to meet me outside. I waited for you."

"Oh. Sorry, babe." He didn't take his eyes off Rob Chang and Nick, one of the other water polo guys, who were taking shots of something out of each other's shoes. Gross. "The flip cup teams were uneven and they needed me for a second. We kicked ass."

"But you told me you were going to come outside and talk to me." A whine crept into my voice. "I told you I needed you, and you left me out there so you could keep getting drunk and groped by Jenny Roy."

"Let's go now," he slurred, grabbing my arm and yanking it. I knew he was drunk, and he didn't mean to be rough with me, but his hand clasped around my biceps still stung. I wrenched my arm loose from his grip. "Sorry, babe," he mumbled. "Didn't mean to grab you like that. Just a little wobbly." He laughed. I didn't.

"I can't talk to you like this," I said. My voice grew louder again. "I told you I really needed you and you just left me sitting out there."

"Babe, chill," he said. "I told you we can go outside now."

"Don't tell me to chill." Everyone in the room stopped

what they were doing and all their drunk eyes turned to us. The music still played loudly and conversations still happened, but we had become a focal point.

I leaned up and whispered, "You told me to talk to you about the personal stuff that's bothering me. I was trying to do that. And this is how you act? When I finally decide to open up?"

I hoped he would whisper back, but instead he replied for the whole room to hear. "You really think the middle of a party is the right time to open up to me about personal stuff?" He laughed, like me trying to talk to him about what I just found out about my parents was up there at "Channing Tatum winning an Oscar" levels of ridiculous.

"Oooh," one of the water polo guys taunted. "She wants to open up to you right now, Curt. You better get on that."

"You need to use my bedroom, Mitchell?" Rob Chang said, and laughed.

My face burned. I couldn't believe this was happening. Curt ditching me was bad enough, but now the whole party was making fun of me.

"Stop it, guys," Curt said, waving his arms around. "Don't talk about my girl like that." But it was too late. They were all laughing. At me.

I tightened my hands into fists and let them out slowly. "I'm leaving."

"What? Why? What's your problem, Kara?"

"She's just wasted," Jenny said from the corner. "You shouldn't listen to her drunk nonsense."

My head snapped over in her direction, and I shot her the dirtiest look I had in my arsenal of stink eyes. "What are you talking about? I haven't had a single thing to drink."

"Whatever." Snark dripped off her tongue.

"She's right," Curt said. "You should have some water and chill out."

"I'm not drunk!" I yelled. "And I can't believe you right now. You're the one who needs to sober up and remember how to be a decent boyfriend." My words to Curt shocked me as they came out of my mouth, but it was true. I'd been to parties with him when he was drinking before, and he'd never been like this. But I'd always been having fun right along with him. I'd never needed him like I needed him tonight. I tried to open up to him, and he let me down big-time. "I'm going. Call me when you get your head out of your ass."

"You probably shouldn't drive like this!" Jenny shouted after me.

I flipped her my middle finger.

Once I was outside and the crisp night air hit me in the face, I started to calm down. A few deep, soothing breaths lowered my anxiety level, and I even considered turning around to go back inside the party and try to talk things out with Curt.

No, I thought. *He'll probably come after me in just a second. It's way better to talk to him out here than inside with all those people watching, anyway. The night air will sober him up, and we can have a normal conversation.*

I leaned against a dirty Jeep parked in the driveway and listened to the sounds of the party still pumping from the house as I waited. And waited.

Curt didn't come.

This was the second time he left me waiting tonight. No, wait. The third, actually. This time he didn't actually tell me he was coming, but I'd assumed. He told his friends not to make fun of me, but he let me run off upset? Really?

Fine, I thought. *I don't need this tonight.*

Fighting back tears, I kicked off my heels and walked barefoot over to my car in the ditch. First my mom told me that my parents were probably getting a divorce, and now my boyfriend let me down twice, let himself get groped by a girl whose mission in life was to replace me like a trash bag, and embarrassed me in front of all his friends. My mind was blown by how much I'd been looking forward to this terrible night, so much that I couldn't even be bothered to worry about what nasty foot fungus I was probably picking up as I traipsed around barefoot.

I buckled myself into my car, and my stomach reacted with one of the loudest growls a human had ever made. I'd gotten so upset with my mom that I didn't grab any pizza before I left the house, and there had been nothing remotely edible in Bob Chang's kitchen. I hadn't eaten anything since my post-rehearsal protein bar. No wonder my stomach was talking to me.

It's not like I could go home yet, anyway. I hadn't been gone long enough to see a movie with Amanda, and I didn't want to make up some story to Mom about why I was home so early. So it looked like a solo date at Taco Bell was in order. And I'd take the super-long way so I could sort through all this drama with a good drive.

Tires screeching, I pulled out of the ditch and got on the road, my mind shuffling through all the facts of the evening.

If my parents were getting a divorce, was I going to have to choose whom to live with? Would I have to go back and forth between them? Would we have to go to court, or was that just on TV?

If Mom's big problem was that she didn't know what job to get or what to do with herself now that she was done raising me, how would she support herself without my dad? Was alimony really a thing? Was there more to this story that I hadn't heard them arguing about?

Was one of them going to get married again? Was I going to have random stepsiblings?

Would they still be able to send me to college?

I felt sort of selfish for a minute as I realized these thoughts were all about me, me, me. But my parents were obviously thinking only about themselves here. Someone in this situation had to think about me.

And what happened with Curt back there at the party? This was a side of him I hadn't seen before. I hated taking off on such a negative note, but he was being such a drunk A-hole, and I had no experience dealing with this version of him.

Even still, I didn't want to leave things like this. I waited until I pulled to a stop at a red light, and I grabbed my phone from the center console.

WE NEED TO TALK. CALL ME WHEN YOU'RE SOBER. XOXO

My thumb hovered over the screen for a second, then I hit Send. Hopefully by the time he sobered up, I would be calmed down. We could talk like two normal people and put our first big fight behind us.

I tossed my phone on the seat as the light turned green. My stomach growled again, and I relaxed at the thought of the burrito waiting for me at the Taco Bell on the other side of the stoplight.

I was halfway through the intersection when there was a crash and an impact.

Glass shattered.

Metal crunched.

And something slammed.

A car. A car, out of control and coming from the other direction, plowed right into the side of my car. Impact. Full force. It didn't stop until it hit me.

I jerked forward, I screamed, I smelled smoke and heard a crash and felt pain shooting through my body.

But before I could make sense of anything that happened, everything went black.

CHAPTER 5

The sounds caused a pull, a tugging sensation from some-where inside me that told me to open my eyes. They seemed to poke at me from far away, sometimes loud, sometimes quiet. Voices in hushed tones, a consistent beeping, the scraping of metal against metal, a shrill squeak.

Then, piled on top of the sounds, there were the smells. The smell of clean. Something medicine-y. Other scents, familiar, but out of context, and something inside me told me to look around and see where I was. I didn't want to open my eyes. It didn't feel like the natural thing to do, and when my eyelids tried to separate, it felt like prying an electric garage door open with my bare hands.

Waking up shouldn't be this difficult, I thought, so I gave up and decided to keep sleeping. Sleep was good. But there was light now, flooding the other sides of my eyelids, bright and welcoming. And the voices started making sense, sounds formed into words, and I knew I had to open my eyes, even though it took so much effort, and I was still so, so tired.

I pried my eyes open and the light was brighter, harsh now, and overwhelming. Squinting, I tried to focus on what was in front of me. I blinked and blinked and blinked in an attempt to focus, trying to make sense of the light and the shapes and the sounds and the smells.

And it slowly started to come together. My parents. It was my parents next to me, saying my name, leaning in close. They seemed excited, clutching each other and sort of freaking out. As all this processed in my head, I wondered, *What the heck are they doing in my bedroom, watching me sleep like this?* The awkwardness made my face crinkle up, and I wanted them gone. But as I blinked more, the rest of the room came into focus. Instead of my dresser and my closet, I saw machines and curtains and plants and ugly wallpaper—all things that told me I wasn't in my bedroom at all.

Where was I?

Mom leaned close and clutched my arm with ferocity, like she needed to make sure I was real. "Kara," she whispered in a soft tone that didn't match her iron grip. "Sweetie. You're awake."

I opened my mouth to reply, but words seemed stuck in my throat. My tongue was dry, and all I could manage was a thick, garbled "heknjd" that scraped on the way out. I wasn't even sure what the word was supposed to be, so I tried again. "Mom." There. At least that was a word. What was wrong with me?

"Oh, thank God," Dad said, and he leaned forward and grabbed my arm, too. "How are you, honey?"

Blinking, I tried again to focus on the room. Nope, definitely not my bedroom. My eyes started to uncloud, but my mind wasn't there yet.

"Where am I?" I finally squeaked out in something that sounded more like a cartoon mouse than my own voice.

"You're in the hospital, sweetie." Mom's voice also sounded nothing like her. She was never this quiet and tentative unless she knew I wouldn't like what she was going to say.

I blinked and blinked and blinked again, trying to break through the thick fog in my brain and my mouth. "Hospital?" My voice sounded a little more solid the more I used it, so I kept going. "Why?"

Dad cleared his own throat and tightened his grip on my arm. "Can you tell us what you remember?" Dad asked. "What's the last thing you remember doing?"

"Sleep," I said. All I could get a handle on was the deep sleep I had just come out of.

From their faces, I sensed that this was the wrong answer, so I closed my eyes and struggled to focus on a memory, something concrete. Something before the sounds and smells and yanking my eyes open to this strange room with my crying parents. After a moment, something flashed through my head.

"Party. Rob Chang's party." It occurred to me as soon as I said it that I never actually told them about the party. Mom thought I had been at the movies with Amanda. I couldn't remember why I was in the hospital, but I could remember that I'd lied to my parents.

"Good," Mom said, and I was relieved she didn't bring up the lie or even look mad about it. "Anything else? Do you remember what happened?"

"Curt. Um, we fought," I said slowly. The memory of our

argument danced around the edge of my mind. I couldn't place what we fought about, but I knew I desperately wanted to talk to him. Had he been here, waiting for me? Was he out in the waiting room or getting coffee? Hopefully he'd be in here soon. And hopefully, like with my mom, the argument wouldn't even really matter anymore, since I was okay now after . . . whatever had happened to me. "I left alone."

"Okay, good," Dad said. "I'm glad you remember all of this."

"Hungry," I said. Cobwebs cleared my head one by one, and details crept in. "Curt and I fought. I left alone. I was hungry. Wanted Taco Bell." A fact popped into my head, one that I felt was very important to tell my parents. "Wasn't drinking," I said. "Only water at the party. Not—"

"We know, sweetie."

"How?" Now that my eyes and my brain were cooperating, I really noticed how haggard my parents looked. Mom was always put together, even for a run to the store, but today her hair was pulled up in a sloppy topknot, her hoodie had a coffee stain on the chest, and dark circles pooled under her eyes. And Dad, in an old UCLA T-shirt and a baseball cap, neither of which had ever been worn outside the backyard, looked as if he hadn't shaved or even slept in days.

Waking up in the hospital was enough of a red flag, but the disheveled state of my parents was the truly alarming thing. My dad loved to tell me how my mom did her whole beauty routine—Velcro rollers in her hair, blow-out, full face of makeup—while in labor with me, contractions and all, because she didn't want to look bedraggled in the "I just had a baby!" photos. Mom didn't do unkempt, so seeing her like this sent a severe sense of dread pulsing through my body. Something was really wrong here.

"The doctors ran a blood test," Dad said. His lips pressed together in a line, like he was attempting to smile, but couldn't quite bring himself to do it. "You're fine. We know you weren't drinking."

I tried to let out a long sigh, but it caused more discomfort than relief. Thanks to the uneasy dread I was feeling, my body wasn't able to relax enough to sigh the way I wanted to. "That's all I remember." The words came more easily now. "Can't remember after I left Rob's house for food. Not a single thing after that." Disappointment crept into my voice; why couldn't I come up with anything useful? Something obviously got me from my car to this hospital room, and it was annoying not to be able to make a single connection between the two. "Tell me what happened."

"Kara, honey." Dad took off his hat, ran his hand through his thinning hair, and returned the hat to his head and his hand to my arm. "The doctor is going to be in here in just a second to explain all of this to you, okay?"

"But I want to know now. Can't you just tell me now?

Dad sighed, and looked at the door. When the doctor didn't magically appear to field this question, he stood up, sat back down again, then stared intently at his knees. "There was an accident. You were in a very bad car accident."

"Accident?"

Dad cleared his throat. "A drunk driver ran a red light and hit your car."

"You're lucky to be alive," Mom said. She patted my arm and stared at me, probably waiting for some sort of reaction. I wasn't sure how I was supposed to react, though. This whole situation was so over-the-top and ABC Family; I had no idea how real-life people reacted to this sort of news.

"Was anyone else in the car?" I thought I remembered

leaving the party alone, but my memory was so shaky that anything could have happened. Was that it? The dread? Did someone die? Curt? One of my friends? "Is everyone okay?"

"You were by yourself in the car," Mom said.

Dad cleared his throat again and his voice got tight. Angry. "And the driver who hit you, he didn't make it."

Process, process, process. A drunk guy ran a red light and hit me while I was driving alone. He died. I'm lucky to be alive. I heard the words, but none of them clicked in my brain. None of them eased the wrongness hanging thick in the air.

"I don't understand," I finally said. I was still blinking repeatedly, waiting for this to make sense. Why didn't I remember being in an accident?

"It's okay, sweetie," Mom said. "The doctor said you probably wouldn't remember everything right away. Your body went into shock to protect itself. It's totally normal."

"We're just so glad you're awake, honey. We've been so worried about you."

"Have I been asleep long?" I didn't feel rested at all. In fact, just talking to my parents was exhausting me, and I couldn't deny that closing my eyes and dozing off sounded more appealing than anything else. I could find out these details later, and maybe after a nap, the dread would ease and this would all make more sense.

Mom and Dad both took their hands off my arm, and through my fluttering eyes I noticed them shifting around on their chairs. I was so sleepy, I didn't even remember exactly what I'd just asked them, but it obviously made them squirm.

"How are you feeling?" Dad asked. "You look tired. You should go back to sleep."

"I don't know." It was all I could think to answer as I

struggled to keep my eyes open. Other than tired and confused, I honestly couldn't get a handle on how I was feeling. Was "let me think about it" an acceptable answer to that question? I was in an accident that almost killed me. I felt like something was terribly wrong, but I didn't know what it was. Shouldn't I be in more pain? Or was that what all these IVs were for? Pumping me full of painkillers?

"I'm going to get the doctor," Dad said, standing up.

"The doctor will be here in a minute." Mom's voice was strained. "You should stay here with your daughter."

"I'll stay with my daughter as soon as I get the doctor," Dad said. "I'll be right back."

Oh, yeah. All this focus on what I could remember had shifted my attention from what I wished I could forget. My parents getting a divorce. The constant fighting. They'd managed to keep it reined in for an entire ten minutes to worry about me as a team, but that didn't last long. Was that why I felt like something huge was wrong?

"Fine. I'll just wait here while you—"

"Stop it. Please." I barely squeaked the words out, but with how quickly my voice silenced the room, you'd think I screamed at full volume.

"Sorry, honey," Dad said, looking at me sheepishly. "I'm just going to run and get the doctor, okay? Then I'll be right back."

Mom watched him go, her eyebrows pulled together so tightly, a deep crease formed above her nose. Then, just like that, her face was back to normal again. "Everybody's been worried about you, honey," she said, obviously desperate to move us both away from the lingering tension of their argument. She leaned forward and brushed my hair from my face with her fingers, a tired smile on her face. "Can you see all the flowers in here?" She cocked her head toward the colorful floral arrangements, small balloons poking out of plants, and cheerful stuffed animals that filled the room. "They're all from your friends at school and the studio. Everyone's going to be so happy to hear that you're awake. Everyone's been praying for you, sweetie."

"Wow," I said, my voice small and quiet.

"See those sunflowers?" Mom said, pointing at a large arrangement by the window. "Those are from the dance studio. And that big one there with the gerbera daisies is from Jack and Amanda. Isn't that sweet of them?"

"Which flowers are from Curt?" Ever since I'd remembered our fight, it was one of the only things my brain managed to focus on. I needed to talk to him. I couldn't stand this feeling of things being unresolved between us.

"Well, sweetie," Mom said, patting my arm again. "Curt has, uh . . . he's been very busy with school and water polo."

"What? How long have I been here?" The dread came to life under my skin. That sinking feeling plus the talking had me more awake, and I remembered my question from earlier. "How long have I been sleeping?"

Mom's eyes darted to the door of my room, as if she hoped someone would come in and keep her from having to answer this question. Too bad she already drove Dad out the door. "It's been about two weeks now."

Her words slammed into me at full force. "What? Two weeks? I've been . . ." My mind reeled again, and I couldn't even seem to form a coherent sentence. I thought I'd been asleep for one night, maybe two. But two *weeks*? I lost the last two weeks of my life?

Two weeks of dance rehearsal gone, and now I'd be behind all the other girls for the recital routine. And what was going to happen to my hip-hop duet? There was no way we could pull it together now with the recital so close. Curt was supposed to take me out to a fancy dinner at the beach to celebrate our nine-month anniversary, but we didn't even get to celebrate. And missing two weeks of school? That was so much homework. So many tests, right at the beginning of the school year. I'd be so far behind. The thoughts of everything I'd missed made the beeping on the machine beside my bed speed up.

And I still had that feeling. The feeling that this wasn't even the worst of it. But something kept me from verbalizing it. I didn't want Mom to confirm that I was right.

"We've been here every day, Kara," Mom said, shooting glances between the monitor and my anxiety-ridden face. "Your dad and I have been sitting right here, praying for you to wake up. It took some time, but your body was healing. And so was your brain."

Dad walked back in the room and cleared his throat once more. "The doctor is coming," he said, and he took his place next to my mom at my bedside. Mom leaned over and whispered in his ear, and this time he was the one with the forehead wrinkle. They both turned to look at me, faces serious and scared, and didn't say anything.

Suddenly I was painfully uncomfortable in this hospital bed with my parents staring at me like some kind of science experiment.

"That's a long time," I said, the panic inside me creeping out through my voice. "Two weeks is a really long time. That's not normal. What's wrong with me?"

"Honey, when the paramedics got to the scene of the accident, they didn't even think you'd survive the ambulance ride to the hospital." Dad's voice was a gravelly whisper, and it was obvious that this was hard for him to talk about. I guess it should have been difficult for me to hear, too, but it still didn't even feel like my life. Maybe I was still in that shock Mom was talking about. "Your body underwent so much trauma. And you had to have an operation on your back. You needed the time to recover. It's okay that you were out that long. In fact, the doctors said it could have been months. We're so glad you are awake now."

I couldn't ignore the dread for another second, not with their tight lips and wrinkled brows. I knew those faces; there was something they weren't sharing with me. Something more than the fact that no one thought I would make it. "So, I'm going to be fine, then? Now that I'm awake, everything is fine?"

My parents shared a look, one I'd seen a million times since I was a kid. It was a look that said there was something they needed to tell me, but they were having a silent argument over which one of them would deliver the bad news.

"Come on," I pleaded. "What are you not telling me?" I tried to brace myself for what could possibly come out of their mouths as the dread pumped through my body. Did they officially file for divorce already? Did I need another operation? How awful could this be?

In an effort to prepare myself to hear their bad news, I moved my arms up and tried to use my elbows to readjust my position on the bed. And as I did that, a tingly feeling spread up and down my arms, like they'd fallen asleep. There was an unusual feeling in my midsection, a definite soreness in my upper back, and . . . that was it.

That was it besides the dread, cold and complete, overtaking my body and my brain, because I couldn't feel anything below the middle of my back.

There was no pain. No tingling. No discomfort at all. Just nothingness on my bottom half, as if my body ended somewhere around my middle.

And I realized slowly, maybe more slowly than I should have, but denial is tricky that way, that I couldn't feel my legs.

At all.

CHAPTER 6

I tried squirming around on the bed, but I couldn't make the feeling come back into my legs. It wasn't the tingly falling-asleep feeling I'd had in my arms. It was a *nothing is there at all* feeling, and it freaked me out in ways I couldn't even begin to explain. The more I moved around and didn't feel anything, the more I panicked. My heart pounded like crazy, sending the monitors I was attached to beeping out of control, and, within seconds it seemed, my room was flooded with nurses and doctors as my parents flailed and cried and I screamed. "My legs!" I screeched as loudly as I could. "What's wrong with my legs?"

People in scrubs and white coats sped around the hospital room, checking monitors and shouting out things to each other and to my parents. One of the nurses came right up to me, rested her hand gently on my shoulder, and leaned over so she was right in my ear. "It's okay, Kara," she said. "Just relax. It's okay."

A doctor scanned my charts and asked my parents questions, and Mom and Dad kept flapping around and trying to answer him and doing their best not to freak out.

Like I was.

All the air I tried to take in caught in my throat, like no amount of effort could get the oxygen to my body. My heart pounded in my chest and in my ears, and I tried to roll myself over, just to see what would happen, but the bed's side rails pinned me in place. I clawed at the tubes attached to me, because this had to be a dream, and I needed to do something to wake myself up.

I couldn't breathe. I couldn't move. And I felt nothing past my midsection. How could I not feel my legs?

I jerked everything on my body I could feel, every way I could, until two nurses held me down. "We need you to get your heart rate down," one of them said into my ear. "Everything will be okay, Kara. You just need to do your best to get calm." I wanted everything to be okay, more than anything ever in the world, so I followed her lead and sucked in as many deep breaths as I could.

Eventually my heart rate slowed back to normal, and the doctor who'd read my chart, a tall Asian guy who was surprisingly young-looking to be a doctor, came to my bedside and smiled at me. "I'm glad to see you awake, Kara. I'm Dr. Nguyen." His tone was a little lighter than the no-nonsense voice I expected from a doctor. "Now, I'm sure you have some—"

"What's wrong with me?" I yelled, panicky and confused. "Why can't I feel my legs?" While I was glad he was cool, I wasn't going to calm down until we dealt with the elephant in the room.

"I'm not sure what your parents have told you since you woke up, but—"

"They told me I was in a car accident. That I've been asleep for two weeks. That's pretty much it."

"I'm sure that was a lot for you to take in," he said. "But there's more I need to tell you. You sustained a spinal cord injury as a result of the accident. Because of that injury to your vertebrae, you've suffered paralysis from the waist down." His jaw clenched, and he said, "I'm so sorry."

What? Paralysis? I was paralyzed? No. That couldn't be right. He had to be wrong. He had to be. Fighting back the tears that welled up in my eyes, I looked over at Mom and Dad for some kind of signal from them that this was a joke. Some slight smile creeping up Dad's face, or a crinkle in the corner of Mom's eyes that would tell me they were playing some horrible, elaborate prank on me. That Dr. Nguyen was actually one the guys my dad worked with, promised an extra day off or something to goof on the boss's daughter. There was absolutely no way that this was real life.

But all I saw on Mom's face was heartbreak. And Dad showed nothing but sadness and grief. They weren't stifling laughter at this epic joke; their faces mirrored exactly what I was feeling inside. Tears welled up in my eyes and hovered there, right on the brink of spilling. I wanted to cry, but the tears held their ground. I pressed the heels of my hands into my eyes and swallowed down the lump forming in my throat; then I pulled my hands away and made every effort to keep myself together.

"Forever?" I asked them, my voice wobbly. But I didn't even wait for an answer. I knew. I'd known the second that feeling of dread crept across my skin when I woke up.

I'd never be able to use my legs again.

Dr. Nguyen was talking about operations and physical therapy and wheelchairs. Recovery and statistics and adaptations. But I wasn't listening. I tuned out after he said "paralyzed," because that was when my life stopped being my life and my future stopped being my future, and I stopped having any idea who I even was.

My eyes closed.

I don't remember going to dance class for the first time, but it was a story my mother loved to tell. She brought me to the intro class for kids at the studio, and I knew the minute I walked in there, at five years old, that it was my new home. I've seen the pictures; I wore a pink leotard and pink tights and tiny pink ballet slippers and my blond hair knotted tightly on the top of my head, secured with a pink ribbon. Mom told me she thought I would be scared. Every time she dropped me off at kindergarten, I cried until I saw Amanda, who was my best friend and attached at my hip from day one, so she thought my reaction to dance class would be more of the same. But instead, when she introduced me to my first dance teacher, I hugged Miss Jana's legs and smiled the biggest smile Mom had ever seen. I stayed right in the front for the entire class, and I cried when Mom tried to take me home.

Even at five years old, I knew I was made to be a dancer. My first effortless pirouette. My first kick into the air, when my leg flew impossibly high. My first routine learned and performed to perfection. Dancing was always in my bones, in my skin, just waiting to come out.

I watched Curt play water polo and I saw how easily it came to him. Treading water while throwing a ball across a pool into the goal and defending himself from the other team. He made it look like it was something he could do in his sleep, even though I knew how much he practiced, how hard he worked for it. Dancing was like that for me. It was my entire life. From five until seventeen. I was going to dance in college. I was going to figure out a way to dance as a job.

That had always been the plan.

Before this. Before some A-hole drunk driver plowed into my car, yanking my dream, my life, the thing I loved away from me.

Dr. Nguyen stopped talking, and when I opened my eyes again, he was looking at me, waiting for me to reply. I'd zoned out so long ago, I had no idea what he'd even been saying.

"I'm a dancer," I told him, as if bringing this fact to his attention would make him realize what a horrible mistake this whole thing was. It's not like I was just some random teenager who lost the use of her legs. I needed to be able to walk because I needed to be able to dance. I needed to be able to dance like I needed to be able to breathe.

Dr. Nguyen looked at me, *really* looked at me, and a flicker of sadness and sympathy passed through his eyes. "I know."

CHAPTER 7

My restless, dreamless sleep was interrupted by voices in my hospital room. I used to be a deep sleeper, able to doze off anywhere and everywhere and sleep like the dead until Mom literally dragged me out from under my covers. But since the accident, since all these nights in the hospital, I woke at the slightest noise. I never felt rested. I never felt comfortable. I never felt like myself.

Today, these voices jolted me from sleep because they were different from the voices I'd grown used to. These voices weren't Mom or Dad, who'd started visiting in shifts. They didn't belong to Dr. Nguyen or any of the nurses I'd gotten to know—Laura during the days, usually, who tried to make me laugh with her terrible corny jokes, and Carmen in the evenings, who told me the plot lines of all the soap operas she watched. No, these voices were new. Not unfamiliar, but not ones I'd heard since I'd been in this room.

"She's awake," Amanda said when my eyes fluttered open. She had her trademark huge smile on her face, that smile that always made me feel better when I was bummed out about something, and her eyes sparkled. Like me waking up right now was the single most miraculous thing she'd ever witnessed.

"Hey, gorgeous," Jack said. He sat next to Amanda, and he wore his normal beanie, even though it was late September in Southern California and probably still surface-of-the-sun hot outside. His hair was a little longer than the last time I saw him over the summer, and blond curls circled around the edges of his knit cap.

It was no surprise that Jack and Amanda were my first nonfamily visitors. They lived next door to each other and they were friends with both each other and me; we'd been quite the trifecta back when Jack and I were dating. But we hadn't been a threesome in almost a year, despite the best efforts of both of them, and being all together again like this gave me both a sense of nostalgia and a feeling of unease.

And I won't even mention my epic disappointment that my first nonfamily visitor wasn't Curt.

"Stop lying." I tried to sound light, like we were chatting over lattes at Starbucks and not uncomfortably gathered in my sterile hospital room. Since they were here, I figured I might as well try to ease some of the awkwardness. "I know I'm a hot mess."

After much begging, Mom finally brought me a mirror yesterday and let me see myself. Trying to prep me for the reality of how I looked, she warned me that I was still healing from the damage of the accident and that, unlike my spine, none of the damage on my face was permanent. Luckily the air bag and seat belt kept my head from smashing through the windshield, but I was still pretty banged up. Cuts from the shattered window, two black eyes from a broken nose, swelling from all of the above. It was surreal looking in the mirror; it was like I was looking at someone else entirely. Because besides the injuries, the person in the mirror looked lost. Empty. There was no light in her eyes, no life in her weak smile. If not for my long blond hair and the small scar I'd always had right above my eyebrow from when Amanda's little brother, Sean, threw a toy truck at my face when we were kids, I'd have never recognized myself in that girl. But what was a swollen, cut-up face and lost-looking eyes when my legs didn't work? At least this would change with time. At least this would heal.

Jack smiled a nervous smile and put his hand tentatively on my arm. It was the lightest pressure, but it was comforting. "You look amazing, Kara. Truly." He let out a small staccato laugh. "Besides, modeling is actually ranked one of the worst jobs for women in America. The average working model only makes like eleven dollars an hour. Looking perfect all the time isn't even worth it."

I rolled my eyes. "How long have you been holding on to that fun fact?"

"We saw pictures of your car," Amanda said, changing the subject. She twirled her long braids around in her hand, a sure sign she was as nervous as I was. "It's a miracle that you survived. When you didn't wake up right away, God, we were so worried. I'm so glad——"

"You're such a rock star for making it out of that accident, Kara. Not everyone would've survived that."

"I didn't do anything special," I mumbled. And I thought,

It's not like I tried to stay alive. And I ended up paralyzed, anyway.

But it occurred to me suddenly that they might not know about my legs.

I pulled my arm out from under the light pressure of Jack's hand. "So, did my parents tell you? About . . ." I trailed off because I hadn't said it out loud yet, and I didn't want to. It was almost like me saying it, admitting it, meant I'd never be able to turn back.

Amanda's eyebrows drew together. She gave me a little nod, and we didn't say anything else. Jack didn't even jump in with a fun fact about how many paraplegics go on to fly to the moon or cure cancer. They didn't want to talk about it. I didn't want to talk about it.

Silence fell over the room.

"Oh," Jack said, and he jumped up from the chair and reached behind him. "We brought you some stuff."

Amanda's sad look fell away, and that big smile was on her face again. "We figured you were probably bored, so we brought you some things to keep you busy."

Jack sat down and balanced a bright green tote bag on his lap, looking so proud of himself. He'd always been pretty enthusiastic about things, much more than the average guy, but I could tell he was laying it on extra thick today for my benefit.

He pointed at the bag. "Books——"

"Trashy ones. Romance novels, not schoolbooks," Amanda was quick to clarify.

"Magazines, a crossword puzzle book, some snacks."

"I was thinking I could paint your nails right now. If you wanted me to."

"I'd help, but that would be weird." Jack smiled. "But I can read to you from this trashy magazine. I hear it says in here that stars are just like us."

The unease I'd felt when I woke up and saw Jack and Amanda sitting there next to me was ridiculous. These two people from my past—the best friend I was growing away from and the ex-boyfriend who was still a friend—nothing was weird with them, and I always seemed to forget that.

I couldn't stop thinking about Curt's conspicuous absence, though. I didn't know why he hadn't come, or why anyone else hadn't come, but I couldn't bring myself to ask. There weren't many things more pathetic than asking someone to find out if my boyfriend was going to bother to show up to visit me in the hospital.

"Thanks, you guys," I said, forcing a smile back at them. "Really."

Amanda smiled, too, as she rustled through the tote bag. "So, hot pink? Lavender? Or black?"

"Let's do the black," I said. "It matches my face."

HEY CURT. I'M AWAKE NOW AND I'D LOVE TO SEE YOU. CAN YOU COME BY THE HOSPITAL? 6TH FLOOR, ROOM 6750.

SOME PEOPLE FROM SCHOOL CAME BY TO VISIT TODAY. I WAS HOPING IT WOULD BE YOU. MISS YOU.

YOU DIDN'T FORGET ABOUT ME, DID YOU? LOL

———

"Do me a favor," I asked Amanda the following day as she sat next to my bed, reading my horoscope from another trashy celeb magazine. ("Changes are afoot for you, Aries." Interesting choice of words.)

"Sure. Anything."

"Can you walk around and tell me who all these flowers and things are from? I feel bad that I don't know."

"Oh, yeah." She bounced up from the chair and walked up to the first arrangement, a small and delicate vase full of Stargazer lilies. "This is pretty," she said. She grabbed the card and read it in a dramatic voice. " 'Dear Kara, Wishing you a speedy recovery. Our thoughts are with you. Best, Dr. Alexander and everyone at Pacific Coastal High School.' Aww, the principal sent you flowers. That's sweet."

"I'm sure it wasn't actually Dr. Alexander. I bet anything it was Mrs. Mehta in the front office. You know she does everything for him."

"Fair enough," Amanda said. "Moving on. Here we have a tasteful arrangement of yellow roses in a clear glass vase." She moved her hands up and down in front of the flowers like she was presenting them on a game show. "And the card. 'Dearest Kara, We are praying for your quick recovery. Hope you are back on your feet soon.' " Amanda made a face and shoved the card back into the flowers. "Ouch."

"Who was that from?"

"Your dad's office."

"I guess they haven't heard the latest," I said.

"Well, these flowers are looking a little wilted. Maybe they sent them when you first got in the accident."

"Yeah, but they didn't even know if I would live at that point. Much less be back on my feet."

"Maybe they are just a bunch of douche bags?"

"That's much more likely. Douche bags who send wilted flowers. Boo on them."

"Next!"

"Next we have this beautiful vase of colorful gerbera daisies, which I can already tell you is from me and Jack and does not have a jerky card attached to it."

"Those are pretty," I said.

Amanda smiled. "Jack picked them out."

I couldn't help but remember the long conversations Jack and I used to have about our favorite things. I told him about so many of the little joys in life that never failed to bring a smile to my face. My jazz shoes with the hole in the toe, the mug I'd made for my mom at a paint-your-own pottery place when I was five, the goofy dance sequence in the movie *(500) Days of Summer.* There were so many favorites I'd mentioned to him over the years we'd been together, how did he possibly remember how much I loved gerbera daisies?

"Our card says, 'We love you, Kara! Love, Jack and Amanda.'"

"Aww, that's sweet."

"Okay, next."

"You don't have to read them all," I told her. I didn't need to hear "praying for your speedy recovery" worded a million different ways, and I certainly didn't want to know if anyone else wished for me to be back on my feet soon. "I just want to know who they're from." What I wanted was to know if Curt ever sent me anything. Mom said he'd been busy with school and water polo, but too busy to go online and order some flowers? Too busy to answer my texts?

"Okay," Amanda said, and she peeked at every arrangement left in the room. "Your grandpa, your aunt Erin and your cousins, your dentist—wow, that was nice—and this one is from your dance studio. Look at this cute card! Aww, and everyone signed it, even the little kids."

She waved the homemade card in my face, and as much as I wanted to look at all the sweet signatures and notes from the dance girls, I couldn't bring myself to focus on it. All I could think about was the fact that I'd been in the hospital for over two weeks now, after getting in an accident so bad that I'd lost the use of my legs, and none of those flowers were from my boyfriend.

I TRIED TO CALL YOU TODAY, BUT YOUR MOM SAID YOU WERE AT PRACTICE. ARE YOU HOME NOW? YOU CAN GIVE ME A CALL ON MY CELL.

YOU KNOW I'M IN THE HOSPITAL, RIGHT?

I'M GETTING WORRIED ABOUT YOU. IS EVERYTHING OK?

Dr. Nguyen, the nurses, and my parents had talked for days now about me learning to use a wheelchair. And I knew it made sense. I couldn't walk on my legs. I needed to get around. A wheelchair would help me do that. Still, my brain was having difficulty processing the reality of a lifetime spent sitting in a chair. Miracle-walking made much more sense in my head.

After a few days of talking about the future of my mobility, Dad came into my hospital room and said, "You ready to be on the move, sweetie?" And for one sad second, I thought that my ridiculous fantasy had come true, that the doctors found a miraculous cure for my spine and I'd be back on my feet again soon, like the jerky card said. A nervous flutter spread through my stomach, and I propped myself up on my elbows, waiting for an explanation. But Dad wheeled an ugly, hospital-issue wheelchair into the room, and I felt my face fall. Of course that was what he meant.

"It's your new set of wheels," he said. He waved his hands over the top of the chair, like I was supposed to be impressed. His enthusiasm was obviously forced, but I appreciated the effort. "Now, this is just a temporary chair from the hospital. We actually ordered a special one that's being custom-built just for you. But Dr. Nguyen thinks you're ready to get out of bed and get moving."

There was something about moving around without my legs that made everything more real, and way more scary. Like getting in that chair was admitting to myself and the world that I was different. I wasn't prepared to do that, to be that person yet.

So instead of being excited over the prospect of getting out of this bed, this room, and moving around, I blinked back the tears that had suddenly appeared in my eyes. I didn't want to cry in front of Dad right now. Not when he was trying so hard. But I didn't want to get in that wheelchair, either.

What choice did I have, though?

"You ready to take her for a spin?" Dad's eyes met mine, and I saw so much there. Care. Exhaustion. Pleading, but sympathy. That combination of emotions in Dad's face made me push the tears back down where they came from for now and force a smile. For his sake.

"Am I going to need a helmet for this thing?" I asked. And for the first time since I woke up in the hospital, we both laughed.

CURT. WHAT'S UP WITH YOU? PLEASE CALL.

Between my parents coming by on their respective shifts, Jack and Amanda, and various other family members, plus the nurses and doctors always in and out of my door, I rarely spent a day in the hospital alone. The nights, though, were a different story. The more I was being weaned off the pain-killers, the harder it was for me to fall asleep, and the more time I spent scrolling to the end of the Internet on my phone in an attempt to turn my brain off and get some quality rest.

One night, after I'd gorged myself on celeb gossip and couldn't stand to read one more article about an actress's post-baby body, my finger hovered over my touch-screen for at least a minute before I let myself type "paraplegic + wheelchair" into the search field.

I was shocked by all the results that popped up, particularly all the videos. People who had filmed themselves moving from their wheelchair to a kitchen chair without help from anyone. Moving from one wheelchair to another.

Even one girl popping wheelies on her chair. People in col-
ored wheelchairs and customized wheelchairs and wheelchairs that had seats covered with funky fabrics. Nothing
like the boring, hospital-issued chair I'd been using.

This world of people out there in wheelchairs was so new
to me. But it was just that, a world. An entire world I'd had
no idea existed, but I was now officially a part of.

Mom wheeled me down the hallway into the elevator and
pushed the 2 button. Getting out of my bed and my room was
liberating. Leaving this floor of the hospital, going somewhere, it was almost like a vacation. But it was strange doing
it via wheelchair, and I still pushed away the fact that I
wouldn't be able to walk out the doors when it was time to go
in a few days, like I really wanted to.

Mom and I fell into silence on the quick elevator ride. She
hummed along with the generic music piped through the
speakers and I let my mind wander, as I'd been doing a lot recently. Dr. Nguyen had put me on some new pain meds, and
these made it hard for me to focus very long, so I often caught
my mind traveling to strange places. This time I thought
about how I used to choose to take the stairs in buildings to
strengthen my legs for dance, and I'd never be able to do that
again. Dance or take the stairs.

The elevator dinged and the door slid open. Mom wheeled
me out, smiling at the nurses and doctors on the floor. "Physical therapy?" she asked the nurse behind the reception desk,
and the nurse pointed to her left.

"Here we are," Mom said, turning me into a spacious room
set up with various tables, machines, balls, and pads scattered

around. Doctors and nurses worked with a few people spread around the open space, but mine was the only wheelchair in the room.

Mom signed me in, and I watched the nurses bend people's legs back and forth and saw people pull on giant, colorful rubber bands between their arms. I felt like I had wandered into some sort of top secret movie stunt room or something, the way everyone seemed so focused on twisting their bodies into odd positions. I had no idea what was happening, but I wouldn't have been surprised to see someone rappel down a wall or launch into a back handspring out of nowhere.

"Sorry, I'm late! Did you wait for me?"

I turned my head and found what I had been hoping to see—another wheelchair. This one was occupied by a dark-haired girl who was a bit younger than me, but who looked a lot more comfortable in it than I did in mine. She looked like she belonged there, like her wheelchair was a comfy throne she lounged in by choice, and she smiled at the nurse behind the check-in desk.

"Oh, hi," she said when she saw me waiting by the door. "I've never met you before. I'm Ana." She smiled this huge, genuine smile, and she waved at me.

I stared back. I didn't smile, I didn't wave, I had no idea how to respond to this girl who was in a wheelchair and seemed to be happy about it. Did not compute.

Luckily, I had Mom with me to keep me from spiraling into total bitch mode. "This is Kara," Mom said on my behalf. "This is her first time in physical therapy."

"Oh, well, you're in for a treat, Kara." Ana had this voice that was so light and airy, it almost sounded like she was laughing when she talked. "They're pretty nice here. But they can hurt sometimes. They tell me it's for my own good, but I don't know if I believe them yet."

She signed herself in and rolled her wheelchair right up next to mine.

"I'm assuming that since it's your first time in PT that the chair is a new development for you?"

I nodded. I still didn't know what to say.

"I've had mine about a month now," she said. "Still getting used to it. But it's okay so far. It's sorta nice to always have somewhere to sit, you know?"

I narrowed my eyes at her. Ana had a ridiculously positive attitude, and the fact that she kept cracking jokes about being stuck in a wheelchair while I'd spent about two hours the previous night crying about it was grating on my nerves.

"You haven't been out of the hospital yet, have you?" she asked, undeterred by my stink eye.

I shook my head. Was it that obvious?

"I was out for a week, but I got an infection and had to come back. Just you wait, though. You're going to get so much sympathetic head tilt out there, you won't even know what hit you."

"What's that?" I was still wary of her perkiness, but I couldn't help but be drawn into this conversation.

"Oh, you'll know exactly what I'm talking about when you get it. I get it a lot, especially when people find out what happened to me."

I opened my mouth to ask, but she kept right on talking.

"I fell off a balcony," she said. "The wood on the railing at my apartment was totally rotted through. I was leaning against it, talking to my friend on the ground after school and—*bam!*—it just snapped in half and I fell off. Three stories up. Half of the railing fell on top of me and cracked my spine."

She said it so matter-of-factly that it shocked me. Wasn't she upset about what had happened to her? That was ridiculously unfair, that she'd never be able to walk again after some stupid accident that wasn't her fault at all. How could she be so calm about this?

"I think I saw this on the news." Mom clicked her tongue. "Such a shame. You're so young."

Ana nodded. "Yup. Sucks, huh? I'm only twelve and I've already had like a zillion surgeries."

Ana and my mom continued talking while we waited for the nurses to get our physical therapy started. I knew I should have joined in the conversation and talked to this very sweet girl who was in a situation so similar to mine. But I just couldn't. It wasn't Ana so much as her attitude. She was so accepting of her situation. She didn't act like a girl whose life was over. She acted almost happy.

We may both have been in wheelchairs, but our hearts could not have been in more different places.

CAN YOU AT LEAST LET ME KNOW IF YOU ARE GETTING MY TEXTS?

I MISS YOU.

CHAPTER 8

My discharge from the hospital was exactly how I'd seen it on TV and in the movies—the nurses always made those TV patients leave in wheelchairs whether they liked it or not. I always wondered if that was a real rule or one of those made-for-TV plot devices, like everyone in a group of friends dating each other because the writers didn't want to add more characters. I guess it didn't matter if it was true in real life, really, because I was leaving in a wheelchair whether I liked it or not.

I thought about that as Laura, my day nurse, wheeled me through the front doors to meet my dad, who was pulling his car into temporary parking to take me home. I let myself daydream that there was some sort of supernatural force field on the door that would magically heal my spine when Laura pushed me through it, that that's the reason the hospital made people go in a wheelchair through the doors, because the real healing didn't take place upstairs. And then I could walk, or skip or grand jeté, to the car, and I'd be as good as new.

Obviously that didn't happen. But it was a nice little day-dream.

Dad stepped out of the car and walked toward me, trying to mask the nerves I could see all over his face with a smile. "You ready to go home, sweetie?"

I nodded, but I also chewed on the tip of my thumb. Yes, I was ready to go home. Ready to sleep in my own bed and cuddle with Logan. Ready not to have machines beeping at me all night. But at the same time, I didn't know if I was ready to face real life with everything so completely different. I didn't know how to live this life that was in front of me. I tried to muster the excitement I should have had about leaving the hospital and going home, but it was difficult when I wasn't walking.

"Okay," he said, trotting over to the passenger side and opening the door. "How are we going to do this?"

"It'll be just like getting on and off the couch," I said. "I think I can do it." Once I'd been introduced to my chair and the doctors and nurses taught me how to get around in it, they also showed me little tricks that would help me get around in the world. They started off by showing me how to get from the floor back to the chair in case I fell or something. But that was the worst because the nurse kept using her legs to demonstrate it to me. Real helpful. From there we went on to learn crazy things like how to navigate my wheelchair backwards down a flight of stairs in case I was on a high floor of a building and the elevator wasn't working. Or how to get from the chair to a couch or a bed by using the strength in my arms as leverage. As a dancer, I'd always been proud of the strength in my legs. I guess it was time to start appreciating other parts of my body.

"Careful, Kara," Dad said. His face had been lined with worry since I woke up two weeks ago, but now the worry was active, crawling all over him like ants on a picnic blanket. He reached forward as if to catch me, like I was in the process of falling to the asphalt, when I hadn't even made a move off my chair yet.

Ignoring him, I rolled myself up to the open door. I took a deep breath and, just as I'd practiced over and over on the couch in the PT room, leaned over to the seat, put down both my hands, transferred my weight onto my arms, then swung my body out of my chair and into the car. It was far from perfect—I landed lopsided on the seat, with half of me sort of falling out the open door and the seat belt digging into my upper back. But I did it. I successfully moved myself from chair to car.

Dad clapped and cheered like I'd just hopped up and ran a relay, and the cynical part of me wanted to tell him to shut up. I was just getting myself in the car. It's not like I was walking. But another, quieter part of me was proud. Proud of this little thing that I could do all on my own, without a doctor or a nurse or a team of specialists helping me out. So I let myself smile as I adjusted comfortably into the seat, lifting my legs with my hands and arranging them in the space under the seat. "Done and done," I said.

Once Dad folded up my chair and stashed it in the trunk, he climbed into the driver's seat, leaned across the center console, and kissed my cheek.

"I'm proud of you, Kara," he said. And I smiled, because I was pretty proud of me, too.

He pulled out of the hospital parking lot and turned the car in the direction of home.

"Where's Mom?" After the first couple of days in the hospital, Mom and Dad started saying they wanted someone to be with me as much as possible, and that was easier when they divided and conquered. But I couldn't forget the fight they'd had the night of the accident, and I knew these separate visits were less about having someone with me at all times and more about trying to avoid spending time with one another. Neither of them had brought up divorce in front of me again, but they weren't exactly lovey-dovey, either.

Dad cleared his throat. "Well, we've made some changes around the house. You know, for you. Your mother is putting some finishing touches on everything so it's all ready."

Anxiety pumped through my veins. I'd had so much change lately, I wasn't sure how much more I could handle. "What kind of changes?"

He grinned. "You'll see when you get home."

He was right. As soon as we pulled in the driveway, I noticed a ramp right there in our front yard, covering the three brick steps that led up to our front door.

"Wheelchair accessible, just for you!" Dad said.

I snorted when I saw the makeshift plywood ramp. "What's the HOA going to say about this eyesore? Doesn't do much for the curb appeal."

My dad sat on the board of our neighborhood's homeowners' association, and he was one of those guys who was obsessed with our house and yard. Last year, he'd launched a full-scale attack against Mr. Anderson across the street when he installed one of those custom fish-shaped mailboxes; Dad claimed it was an eyesore that was driving down our property value. I wondered if the Andersons would see this hideous homemade ramp as a chance to retaliate.

Dad let out a humorless laugh. "Oh, don't worry. I got it all cleared by the board."

Of course he did. I never should have doubted that he had all his bases covered when it came to the association.

I was out of the car and into my chair much more smoothly this time, and I turned down Dad's offer to push me up the ramp in favor of wheeling myself up without his assistance. The plywood ramp sagged under the weight of my chair, and Dad's arms were outstretched, ready to catch me if the whole thing buckled. "I got it, Dad," I said, pushing myself up the steep ramp.

It was a struggle, but I made it. "I don't know if that should go over the stairs," I said at the top, panting and out of breath. "I feel like I'm pushing myself up at a ninety-degree angle."

"Noted," Dad said. "One more thing I didn't really think about. I can add that to the very lengthy list. We'll get one built for you, how about that? Maybe inside the garage. That should be easier." He swung the door open for me, and I pushed myself in. "We're home!" Dad called as he followed me into the house.

At the sound of Dad's voice, Logan came bounding into the entryway.

"Little Lo!" I said. "I missed you so much, doggie!"

Logan stopped to sniff my chair. Once he decided it met his approval, he leaped up onto my lap, tail wagging, and licked my face like it was a giant pork chop.

Dad lifted Logan from my lap and held on to him while he called again for my mom.

"I'm in Kara's room," Mom called back. But her voice

wasn't coming from my room upstairs; it was coming from my dad's office down the hall.

"Okay, so don't freak out," Dad said. "But we obviously couldn't install an elevator in the house. So we figured the most sensible thing to do was move your bedroom down here."

"You moved my room?" My mind traveled to my secret stash of sexy bras and underwear that were totally inappropriate for parents' eyes, and the journal shoved between my bed and the wall, which was even more inappropriate. My parents had gone through my bedroom? They had touched everything? Nothing good could come of that.

Without thinking, I pushed myself down the hall toward my dad's office. But once I was out of the entryway, I was on the shaggy carpet of the hallway, and as soon as my wheels touched that carpet, pushing myself became much, much harder. "Argh," I said. "This carpet." I used all the force in my arms to push myself forward, and it worked, but it was slow going compared to the ease of the slick floor of the hospital and the tile of our entryway.

"Thick carpet," Dad said. "That's going on the list, too. Sorry, kiddo."

"It's fine," I said. "Just give me—"

"No problem," Dad said. He came up behind me, dropped Logan into my lap, and pushed my chair into the room.

I hadn't been asking for help; I'd been asking him to give me a minute to do it on my own. But he was super quick to assume I needed his assistance. I was about to snap at him, tell him to leave me alone and let me do it, but we were in the office before I even had a chance.

"Yeah," he said. "That carpet is rough. Maybe we'll get

some of those plastic things they put under desk chairs. You know those plastic things?"

He kept rambling on about the plastic things, but I was too distracted by the sight of my mom standing in the middle of my dad's office, which was now my bedroom set up exactly as it had been upstairs. The office was smaller, and it was more rectangular instead of square, but aside from that, it was identical. Mom had even painted the walls the same bright pink and hung my dance posters in their same spots on the wall.

My first reaction was a deep irritation that surged underneath my skin. She rifled through all my stuff without permission. She opened every drawer, touched every box, looked in every secret nook to get this room re-created exactly as it had been upstairs. Before getting in an accident that jacked up my spine and left me paralyzed, I would have said that *this* was my worst nightmare.

But one look at Mom's face told me to keep that irritation to myself. She didn't look like herself at all. My tiny mom looked even smaller, curled into herself somehow. Shrunken. And even though her hair was styled and her face was made up, she still looked unkempt somehow. Worn down. Aged.

So I bit my tongue and kept my irritation inside, under my skin. "Wow," I said. That pretty much covered it.

I rolled my chair over to Mom so I could hug her, but as I got close, she backed up a couple of paces. Turning toward my desk, her back to me, she said, "I tried to get everything exactly as it was. And don't worry, I didn't snoop or anything." She opened the top to my computer, blinked absently at the screen, and shut it again. She was probably lying about the snooping, but just hearing her say it calmed my nerves.

"I love it, Mom. Thank you." Again, I pushed myself closer to her, and again, she moved away. This time toward the closet, where she opened the door and showed me where everything was, even though she'd taken care to put everything in the exact spot I'd chosen for it upstairs, only on a lower bar.

I looked over at Dad to see if he noticed Mom scooting away from me, putting distance between us like my injury was contagious, but he had wandered out of the bedroom. He probably ran off to order a custom crane to lift me around the house.

Mom explained where everything was in my room and told me things I needed to know to go back to school the next day, but she didn't actually look at me, and every time I moved myself toward her, she shifted away.

Eventually I gave up trying to break through to my mom. I sat still as she talked to me about my new bedroom, and I scratched Logan between his ears while he stretched himself out in my lap and licked my arm. It looked like my dog was the only one in this family who could manage to look at me.

I couldn't sleep. Logan was cuddled up next to me, right in the crook of my arm, and I stared up at the ceiling in the dark, trying not to think too hard about how school was going to go the next day. Did people know I was coming back tomorrow? How would they act toward me?

And what about Curt? He hadn't replied to a single one of my calls or texts. Every time I thought about how he'd completely abandoned me when I needed him the most, I got so angry, I felt like my skin was going to light on fire. But I had so much to be angry about that I found myself having to move on and focus my anger elsewhere. I knew I'd see him at school, though. I thought briefly about texting to let him know I was coming back, or texting one of our mutual friends to try to dig for information, but I decided against it. None of those friends had visited or called, and he was obviously avoiding me. If he didn't know I was coming, I had the element of surprise working in my favor. I could finally get him alone and find out what's been going on.

I wanted a distraction from all these thoughts in my head. I was about to pick up my phone and watch some more videos of people doing awesome things in wheelchairs when the door to my bedroom squeaked open.

"Dad?"

"Oh, sorry, honey. I didn't mean to wake you."

"It's fine. I couldn't sleep."

"Me neither." He shuffled over to my bed in the dark and lowered himself down on the edge of my bed. The disturbance woke Logan, who walked himself down to the edge of the bed, curled back up, and was snoring again within seconds.

"Why not?"

I could see him shrug in the dark. "Just thinking about you going to school tomorrow. You ready for this?"

I would have just given a little nod, but I knew he couldn't see me with the lights still off. "It's not like I have a choice, right?"

Dad reached up and patted my arm. "You're so strong, kiddo. I'm so proud of you."

"People keep saying I'm strong," I said. "But I don't get it. I'm not strong. I'm just doing what I have to do. What other choice do I have?"

"That attitude of yours is exactly what makes you strong. There are some people who just give up, Kara. They don't try."

"I can't imagine giving up."

"I know it's hard to see it right now, honey, but this happened to you for a reason. And there's a reason it happened to you and not someone else."

I'm glad he couldn't see me roll my eyes. If I heard that everything happened for a reason one more time, I swear, I was going to wheel myself off a cliff.

"I can tell you're rolling your eyes at me. Just because it's dark doesn't mean I don't know what you're doing." Dad scooted himself around on my bed so that he was able to lean his back against the wall, and Logan, disturbed again by all the movement, walked back up the bed and settled next to Dad with an exasperated grunt. Dad absently stroked his fur. "I know this is nowhere near the same as what you're going through, but do you remember when I told you about tearing my ACL?"

I nodded onto his shoulder; I'd heard this story many times over the years. My dad had a full scholarship to UCLA to play soccer, and he tore his ACL the summer before his freshman year while messing around playing rugby with his buddies in the park. He lost his scholarship and never played soccer competitively again, all because of a random pickup game.

"But even though I lost my scholarship, I still went to UCLA. I didn't give up and stay at home, even though I wanted to. I still got a great education, and I met your mom in a class I would never have taken as a soccer player. If I played soccer, I'd have a different job now, and I wouldn't have you. There's no way I would go back and change what happened to me, even if it meant I'd never been hurt."

"But you could still *walk*, Dad. You still had a normal life. This isn't the same. What good things can possibly happen for me like this?"

He let out a long sigh and reached over to pat my arm. "It's too soon to tell just yet, sweetie. But I promise, good things can and will happen to you. Maybe you'll never walk again, maybe you will. But no matter what, you're still the same Kara Moore. You have awesome things ahead of you."

"I don't feel the same," I said. "Dr. Nguyen has me on so many drugs, my head feels like a cotton ball." I'd been handed a long list of pills to take, to manage things like chronic pain, muscle spasticity, and even depression, which the psychiatrist who'd visited me a couple of times in the hospital thought I might be showing signs of. It was quite the powerful cocktail, and they said they'd adjust the dosages as we went along, depending on my reaction to everything, but I couldn't imagine how I could feel like myself again when I was pumped full of so many meds.

"That feeling will fade with time," Dad said. "You'll be feeling like yourself again soon. I promise."

"Thanks, Dad," I said. I scooted myself as close to him as I could get without crushing Logan and let out a sigh. I didn't know if I believed him or not, but I appreciated him trying. "I still don't want to go to school tomorrow, though."

"Oh, I don't blame you," he said, and laughed. "Every day in college I had to go to campus knowing I should be playing soccer, and seeing all my friends on the team and knowing they had what I should have. It sucked, but I did it. And some people probably would have said I was strong. But it didn't feel like strength to me. It just felt like survival."

I smiled at my dad in the darkness, glad I had someone who understood me a little bit, and I reached over and grabbed his hand. He squeezed my fingers and I squeezed back.

He leaned over and kissed me on my cheek. "This is the toughest thing you'll ever have to go through, sweetie. But your true character comes out during hard times like this. These trials that the universe throws our way, well, they show who we really are."

I was quiet for several long seconds. "What is it showing about me?" I whispered.

"It's showing me that you aren't going to give up. Not for anything. And you know your mother and I are here for you, no matter what."

Tears welled up in my eyes as he gave me another kiss on the cheek and stood up.

"Hey, Dad," I said quietly as he reached for the door. "Are you and Mom going to get a divorce?"

They hadn't said anything more about it after that night, and Dad's stuff was still in the house. There were no more nights at Uncle Kevin's, but I noticed a few extra blankets folded next to the couch that were never there before, and I could tell there was something more than my wheelchair that wasn't here before my accident.

Dad was silent for a long time, and even in the dark of my room I could see his hand hovering over my doorknob. Finally he cleared his throat and said, "I don't know, sweetie."

I'd been expecting a more definitive answer, but the fact that he didn't say yes filled me with so much relief that I relaxed back into my pillow. Since we were on the topic, I considered bringing up Mom's odd, distant behavior, but I didn't want to drag any more drama into our father–daughter time. "Okay," I said. "Good night, Dad."

He walked back to me and kissed me on the forehead, then scratched Logan again. "Tomorrow is going to be tough, but you're so strong, you don't even realize how strong you are. Strength just feels normal to you. You can do this." He walked back to the door, then turned around, facing me in the dark one more time. "Good night, honey. I love you."

Dad's words turned over in my head as I closed my eyes and tried to fall asleep. I didn't feel strong. I felt scared and lost and very, very uncertain about what life was going to be like for me. But maybe simply getting up in the morning was an act of strength. Maybe showing up for school tomorrow, knowing everyone would stare at me, knowing I'd rather be at home in bed, was the strongest act in the world.

CHAPTER 9

For the first time since the accident, I dreamed about dancing. I stood alone on a stage, and the auditorium was completely packed with people. Unfamiliar music played, softly at first and then it grew louder, and I was frozen. I didn't know a routine to this song, that changed from slow to fast and back to slow again, and I wasn't even sure what I was supposed to be doing. I was about to sneak off the stage, but someone in the crowd clapped. The clapping was slow at first, but it picked up speed and spread until the whole audience was applauding for me, cheering and screaming. Prompted by the enthusiastic crowd, somehow, my body knew what to do. I started dancing to the music, and every move was perfect. I didn't remember learning the routine, but I knew it like I knew my name and my family. I danced it like I'd been dancing it my entire life. It made me feel full. Happy. When I was done, the crowd stood up and yelled for me, and I took a bow.

Then I woke up.

The memory of the dream, of being on my feet, dancing across the stage, filled me with a joy and a sense of who I was that felt unfamiliar as I opened my eyes, and for a second I couldn't remember why. But somewhere in that murky place between asleep and awake, reality hit.

I'd never dance like that again. It was just a dream.

The dream stayed with me as I went through my morning routine. Getting around the house in my chair was still a cumbersome and clumsy task, but I managed to take care of everything I needed to do to get ready for school with minimal help from Mom. I even had the time to curl my hair and put on makeup, which I hadn't bothered to do since the night of the accident. I wasn't feeling totally like my old self, like the Kara of my dream, but it was amazing what a little lip gloss and mascara could do.

Once I wheeled out into the kitchen, ready to go, Mom was waiting there for me with a breakfast smoothie.

"Breakfast of champions?" She placed the smoothie on the edge of the kitchen table next to my morning pills and, without really looking at me, went back to whatever else she had going on in the kitchen.

"Thanks," I said. I'd been craving a bowl of Lucky Charms, but I wasn't going to complain. I grabbed the smoothie, popped the pills in my mouth, and washed them down with a big, icy gulp. "Not like I'm in a hurry or anything, but when are we leaving?"

She stopped her cleaning and turned around, a hesitant smile on her face. "So, I have a surprise for you. I'm not taking you to school today."

"Let me guess. I'm driving myself?" I snorted into my

smoothie at my own joke. I'd give anything to be able to be behind the wheel again, and I could use a good drive around the neighborhood right now to calm these back-to-school nerves.

"Jack is coming to get you in about ten minutes."

I watched her face as she said this, bracing herself for impact as she said Jack's name. Yes, Jack and I were doing a great job at the whole "friends" thing, and I'd seen more of him in the past few weeks than I had in the past year, but he was also my ex-boyfriend. And my mom making plans for my ex to drive me to school was more than a little awkward.

"Is that okay with you? He called the house earlier, and I figured it would probably feel less weird for him to drive you."

It was fine. Really, it was. But I guess some part of me had been looking forward to the time in the car with my mom. Why didn't she want to talk to me, really talk to me, the way Dad did? Last night I'd drifted off, giving myself a pep talk, promising I'd ask Mom about why she was being so distant and what was going on with her and Dad. But another chance to talk was gone. Again. It looked like she'd jumped at any available opportunity to avoid me.

So, yeah, even though my mom had been distant and detached and acting like direct eye contact would shatter me like a porcelain doll since I came home from the hospital, she practically crawled out of her skin when Jack came to the door to take me to school. I wouldn't be surprised if it was actually her who called him instead of the other way around.

There was a time that Jack was as constant a feature in my house as my mom's famous Chicken Parmesan. He ate dinner with us almost every night, he played video games with my dad, he helped my mom clip coupons, he even came over and walked Logan when the three of us went on family outings. My parents were definitely more upset than I was about our breakup. I could tell they wanted to be supportive toward me and take my side, but it was obvious how much they would miss Jack around the house every day. I'd almost been tempted to tell them some horrible lie about him—he kicked puppies, he set fire to the school, he stole from the offering plate at church, anything to taint the golden-boy image they had in their minds. I didn't, of course, but I'd so wanted to.

"Why did you ring the doorbell?" Mom said, ushering Jack into the house when he arrived. "The doorbell is for strangers."

"Oh, I didn't know if that was still okay," he said. "It's not like—"

"That doesn't matter. You're always family here."

I rolled out to the front room, Logan trotting along next to my chair. "Want me to find another ride to school so you two can be alone?"

"Good morning to you, too," Jack said. To his credit, he didn't look through me like he didn't know me or stare at me like I was a circus animal or freeze up. He was acting more normal about this whole wheelchair thing than my own mother. Score one for the ex. "You look really great."

"Yeah, except for this whole—"

"Stop it, Kara," Mom snapped. "Jack was being nice to you. Just say thank you and leave it at that."

I'd never been the best at taking compliments. I loved getting attention onstage when I was dancing, but personal, one-on-one attention made me feel all squicky. And now, getting compliments while I was in this wheelchair, how would that work? How would I even know people were being sincere and not just feeling sorry for me?

I doubted anyone else besides Jack would be complimenting me anyway.

"Thanks, Jack," I said, staring at my legs.

He leaned down to pet Logan and looked up at me. "You ready to go? We still have to go back and pick up Amanda."

I brightened at the mention of her name. "Amanda's coming with us?"

"Yeah. She wanted to be with you on your first day back. I hope that's okay."

"Of course it is." We were all just standing around awkwardly in the front room—well, they were standing, anyway—and Mom was gawking and not saying anything, and I wanted to get the hell out of there. "Let's go."

Jack walked around my chair and started to push me, but I snapped at him. "I can do it myself."

"Oh," he said. "Sorry, just trying to help."

"I'll let you know if I need it. How about that?"

"Why don't you grab Kara's book bag? It's right there by the door." Mom's voice was sticky sweet, like she wanted to make sure Jack wouldn't change his mind about driving me after I snapped at him, forcing her to actually deal with me. Oh, the horror.

"Bye, Little Lo. Bye, Mom," I said, not even looking at her. I knew I was having more attitude than I should, but she'd started it by acting so weird. I was supposed to be able to count on my parents to treat me like a normal person. But I also should have been able to count on my boyfriend, and look at where that left me.

"I have your backpack," Jack said, and he opened the door. "Bye, Mrs. Moore."

"Bye, Jack," Mom said. "Bye, Kara. Have a great day."

"Doubtful," I mumbled as I pushed myself out of the house, down Dad's rickety makeshift ramp, and down to the driveway.

Jack tossed my backpack in his trunk, and he stopped to look at me as I sat there next to his Civic. "Oh," he said. He swung the passenger door open and, before I even knew what was happening, he leaned down to wrap his arms around my shoulders and under my legs, our foreheads bonking together.

"Ouch! Jack! What are you—?"

"Sorry. I didn't mean . . ."

I thought he was backing up, but instead he moved his head to the other side and leaned over again, and this time as he reached around me, his hand grazed my boob. Then he yanked it back like he'd touched an open flame.

"Ack!" I screeched.

"Oh my God. I'm sorry. I didn't mean—"

"What on God's green earth are you doing?"

He straightened himself up and looked at me, his face red. "I was trying to lift you into the car."

I didn't mean to laugh so hard. I really didn't. But the whole situation was so ridiculous, I couldn't help it. When I could finally look at him with a straight face, I managed to say, "Do I look helpless? I can get in the car myself, you dork. You don't have to do that." Was my life now going to be filled with people trying to help me all the time?

Jack seemed honestly surprised. "You can?"

"God, just ask, okay? Now, out of the way. Let me show

you how this is done." Just as I had done on my way home from the hospital, I used my arms to lift myself up from the chair and plop myself down in the seat. "Voilà!"

Jack let out an impressed whistle.

"I'm not as helpless as I look," I told him. "But you can go ahead and fold up my chair and toss it in the backseat if you want to feel useful."

He looked from one side of my chair to the other, then sort of flipped himself over and looked at the bottom of it. "How do you—?"

"Right there," I said, pointing at the lever he needed to grab to collapse it. It was a relief to be the one telling people how to use the chair instead of the other way around. "So, were you seriously planning on lifting me, Chicken Arms?"

"Look, I know I don't play water polo or anything, but that doesn't mean I'm totally useless when it comes to acts of brute strength." He winked as he leaned over my chair and folded it up. "Playing Halo really works the ol' biceps, you know?"

Jack stowed my collapsed chair in the back of his car with my bag, slammed the trunk, and hopped in the driver's side of his car. "Off to get Amanda," he said, backing out of my driveway. "I texted her before I left and she was still in pajamas, so hopefully she's had ample time to get herself ready."

We drove in silence for a minute or two with only the morning team on the radio as noise between us. Finally, I said, "Thank you."

"Oh, it's no problem," he said. "You know your house isn't out of the way or anything, so I might as well—"

"No, I mean . . . well, yeah, thanks for the ride. But thanks for being . . ." I couldn't figure out exactly how to say what I wanted to say. Thanks for being there when I was in the hospital. Thanks for bringing me movies and trashy magazines and my favorite flowers. Thanks for collapsing my wheelchair like it's no big deal. "Thanks for being normal." I let out a long sigh. "I have a feeling I'm not going to be getting a lot of that today."

"I doubt people will be as weird as you think they're going to be."

"Of course they are. Didn't you see my mom?"

He gave an uncomfortable, humorless laugh. "I wasn't going to say anything. I thought she was just being strange because I was there."

"Nope. It's because I was there. She's been all distant and not herself ever since I got home from the hospital. And she's my mother. If my own mom can't be normal around me, how are all the randoms at school going to be?"

We pulled up in Amanda's driveway, and she bounded out the front door, her long braids flapping behind her, and she jumped into the backseat of Jack's car. "Good morning, friends! You ready for school, Kara?" Amanda had always been a morning person, and it used to piss me off because I could never muster this much enthusiasm before the clock hit double digits. Today, though, I welcomed her chirpiness as a distraction from my overwhelming dread.

"You need to settle down," Jack said as he pulled the car back onto the street and headed toward school. "It's school, not Disneyland."

"Nothing wrong with being high on life," she said. "Right, Kara?"

"I wouldn't know," I mumbled. It wasn't just that I was heading to school for my first time since the accident; it was that I was heading to school for the first time in almost a year without Curt. His absence left me feeling just as hollow inside as my spinal cord injury did.

"I had a feeling you were going to be a little down this morning." She rummaged through her bag and pulled something out. "Here, this is for you." She reached over the seat and dropped something into my lap. It was a small stuffed bear wearing a T-shirt with a picture of me and Amanda from fourth grade screened on the front. Amanda and I got the peach-colored bear, which we named Patrick after our favorite *SpongeBob* character, at a street fair in elementary school, and we passed it back and forth anytime one of us needed cheering up. I hadn't seen Patrick in years, but the sight of him in my lap as I was so full of anxiety about going to school, well, it was just what I needed. I took one look at it and burst out laughing. Like, snorting, ugly, hysterical laughter. I hadn't laughed that loud or that heartily in so long, I couldn't even remember when. It was before the accident, that's for sure. Before the chair. Before my legs. Nothing since I'd woken up in the hospital had made me laugh like this little bear.

It was a relief to laugh again. I'd wondered if it was going to happen, and I'd spent quite a few lonely nights in the hospital drowning in my feelings, convinced that nothing from that point on would ever make me happy again. How nice to be proved wrong so soon.

Unfortunately, my light mood slipped away as we pulled into the school parking lot. It had been almost a month since I was last here, and even though it was obviously the same school filled with the exact same people, it felt completely foreign. I knew how to get to all my classes, but would I be

able to go my familiar route in my wheelchair? It never occurred to me if there were stairs or bumps or anything that
would prevent me from following my usual path to and from
classes. And the people I knew, those familiar faces . . . how
would they act? Would they be normal, like Jack and Amanda?
Would they be weird like my mom? Would they treat me like
I was completely helpless like my dad? Would they ignore me?
I wondered what would be worse—being treated differently
or being treated like nothing had changed.

"Okay," Jack said. "You ready for this?"

"No," I said, handing Patrick back to Amanda. "Let's do
something else. I'm totally down to go back home and go to
bed. Or we could make a blanket fort. That sounds pretty
awesome right now."

Amanda leaned forward over the seat. "I know you want
to go hide right now. And I don't blame you. But you are
stronger than that."

I bristled at Amanda saying I was strong, just as I had
when Dad said it last night. I wasn't being strong. I was just
going to school. I needed to. My doctor's note was expiring,
and I was already a month behind. I had to graduate at the
end of the year.

This wasn't strength. It was necessity.

I didn't say anything, though. She was taking the time to
be here for me, and she had been since I woke up in the hospital, since before the accident, actually, even though I'd been
keeping her at arm's length. I couldn't snap at one of the few
people who was actually supporting me.

Instead I said, "Fine, let's go." Not for the first time, I
wished I could just step out of the car and stomp off, but I had
to wait for Jack to get my chair from the back of his car and

lock it into place before I could lift myself out. All settled in, I grabbed my backpack from Jack's outstretched hand and arranged it in my lap. I could have hung it from the back of my chair, but I liked having it in front of me, like a shield from the world, one I could hide behind.

This time it was Amanda who was impressed with my maneuvering. I'd have to remember to tell her about the awkward boob-grabbing incident later.

The three of us headed through the parking lot toward school. We passed through small groups of students lingering by their cars before class started, and I noticed eyes following me as I wheeled myself through the unevenly paved lot. I'd always been irritated by the loose gravel and bad paving job in the parking lot, but it had never been more than a general annoyance. Now that I was trying to wheel myself over the top of it, though, it was making my life downright miserable. My arm strength had improved significantly just in the past week or so of using my chair—I was getting some major biceps—but it still wasn't all that great. I was a dancer, after all, and my strength was in my now-useless legs.

I hit my first major snag when I got to the front of the fenced-in parking lot. The lot had a large chain-link fence all the way around it to keep students from wandering off campus. The only way I've ever known to get from the lot to campus was through a small opening in the gate right by the front; all the students filed through this one opening before and after school. I'm not sure if I realized it first or if Jack did, but we both stopped in our tracks, him walking and me pushing, while Amanda kept right on walking through the gate. When she realized we weren't behind her, she turned around and looked at us. "What?"

I watched Jack look at her like she was a complete idiot, and I turned back to her to see realization cross her face. "Oh, no," she said, her face falling. "You don't fit."

Sure enough, my chair was too wide to fit through the narrow opening in the gate. The three of us searched around for another way to exit the parking lot aside from the entrance that we drove into from the street, and we didn't see anything. Unbelievable. I'd made it all the way to school, and now I was trapped in the parking lot.

"Do I seriously have to go all the way around? Are you kidding me?" My voice was shrill, and I knew I sounded whiny, like a little kid who was being told to go to sleep when everyone else got to stay up, but seriously? I couldn't fit through the gate everyone walked through? I'd have to wheel myself back across this bumpy asphalt only to have to come all the way around on the sidewalk? That was ridiculous.

"Oh, look," said Jack, pointing about fifty feet down from where we were lurking. "There's an opening right there."

"Is it locked?" Amanda asked.

"Let me go check," Jack said, and he jogged off.

I looked up at Amanda. "The bell is going to ring soon. Don't stand around with me. Just go to class."

She smiled back at me. "Don't be silly."

"It's open," Jack called, waving us over toward the opening. I wheeled over to the gate he was holding open. "A secret door. Who knew?"

A group of people on the other side of the parking gate had stopped to watch me figure out how to get through, like I was some kind of circus act performing for their entertainment. "What are they looking at?" I mumbled.

"Don't worry about them," Amanda whispered back. "They're just curious."

I wanted to say about a hundred different things, but I knew Amanda wouldn't understand. She didn't know how it felt to have the most basic conveniences taken away. She didn't know how it felt to have people stare at you for just trying to get to class.

Once I was out of the parking lot, I was back on sidewalk that was much easier to maneuver over than the bumpy asphalt. But a smooth surface didn't mean a smooth journey to class. Now eyes followed me all the way to first period, coming at me from every direction. People looking. People talking. Jack and Amanda talked up a storm as they walked on either side of me, but I couldn't listen to them when I could feel everyone I pushed past, people I didn't even know, had never spoken to before, staring at me. I figured my accident had become news at school, so freshmen, new students, people who'd never seen me before probably knew who I was now. But these stares. They made me feel like a zoo animal on a campus where I used to blend right in.

I tried to focus on what Jack and Amanda were saying, but it was almost impossible while trying to do two other things at once. One, avoiding all the staring eyeballs as I wheeled down the walkways, and two, keeping on high alert for Curt. I knew he usually hung out around the pool before school, since he had morning water polo practice. As we went by the pool, I slowed down so I was behind Jack and Amanda, and I scoured the area. I didn't see him at all, but I didn't see any of the water polo guys, either, so maybe they were still in the locker room or something.

Of course, though, because this morning had to be as annoying and difficult as possible, I did see Jenny Roy.

She was typing furiously on her phone as she walked out toward the parking lot while Jack, Amanda, and I headed in toward school. Knowing Jenny, she was probably planning to ditch first period and plot evil schemes with the devil himself over mochas at Starbucks or something. As soon as I caught sight of her, I felt my posture fall. Without even meaning to, I curled myself back into my chair as much as I could while still moving myself forward. But trying to slip by unseen was pointless. One thing that had been made clear to me already was that there was no way to make myself invisible.

It took only a few moments for her to notice me, and as she slipped her phone in the back pocket of her shorts, our eyes met. I braced myself for an eye roll or a snarky comment, but I got nothing.

Well, it wasn't nothing. Her eyes passed over me, from head to chair, and something flickered across her face.

Pity, I thought. It looked like she felt sorry for me.

Then, right as we crossed paths, she brought up the side of her mouth in an attempt at a half smile and she shrugged and just kept on walking. No stink eye. No comment. Nothing.

Was Jenny Roy making a truce with me? Was I not even worthy of her disgust and disdain now that I was disabled?

I knew I should have been relieved that the person who never missed a chance to stab me in the front completely passed over an opportunity to be the first to make an issue about me being in a wheelchair. But instead of relief, it was a choking sadness that filled my throat.

I was actually upset that Jenny Roy didn't toss a snarky comment my way, because that meant that I was Different now. And everyone was going to treat me that way.

"Well, here you are," Amanda said as we came to a stop

in front of my first-period English class. We'd crossed the entire campus, and I didn't even realize it. "And I'm all the way across campus for AP Physics, so I'll see you later. You'll rock this." She leaned over, hugged me, and darted off into the sea of students in the hallway before I could say good-bye.

I watched her dark braids bob out into the crowd, and I turned to Jack and shuddered. "Do I have to?"

"According to the State of California, yeah, you do," Jack said, patting me sympathetically on my arm.

"Don't leave," I blurted out as he walked off to his own first period. He stopped in his tracks and turned slowly back to face me. "Stay with me, Jack. Please. Change your class schedule." I'd tried to sound light, like I was totally joking, but my dread at facing this class alone, at being Different without anyone to help me deal, had totally crept out in my voice.

"I wish I could," he said, his mouth turning up in a sad smile. "I really do. But you'll be fine. I promise. And text me if you need anything, okay? One of the privileges of being a Student Government officer is that teachers believe me when I say there's some kind of school emergency and I need to leave in the middle of class. I'll come find you, wherever you are."

He turned to walk, but at the last second he turned back and, like Amanda, leaned over and hugged me. But his hug was tighter and longer and I didn't want to let him go. I didn't want to be alone.

I watched him walk away until he, too, was absorbed by the crowd, and then I gave myself a quick mental pep talk and wheeled into English class, where I was faced with Obstacle of the Day Number Two. Where do I sit? My assigned seat had been directly in the center of the classroom. But with over thirty students and desks packed into this small room, there was no way I could maneuver through this maze. And even if I could get through to my assigned seat, it's not like I could get myself into the desk with its attached chair.

Well, this was awkward.

And to add to the fun, the tardy bell rang just as I was entering the classroom. Which meant the room quickly filled up with students. Students who hadn't seen me since before my accident and had no idea I was going to be back in school today.

Of course, everyone stared as I wheeled to the front of the classroom to ask my teacher, Mr. David, what I was supposed to do. Mr. David had been my least favorite teacher since the first day of school, which was too bad, because I usually liked English. But he established almost immediately that he had no idea how to talk to any of us like we were normal people, and not a day had gone by in class that he hadn't seemed to go out of his way to say something insensitive and insulting to at least one person in class. In the few weeks we'd spent together before my accident, he'd made a comment about how girls just pretend to enjoy sports to impress guys; said gay people could do whatever they wanted, he just didn't want to hear about it; and referred to Kristina Lin as "Oriental."

He was pretty much a walking, talking insult to everyone who wasn't straight, white, male, and ignorant, and no one could understand how he still had a job. I was so not looking forward to his reaction to my wheelchair.

His back was to me as he scribbled the agenda on the whiteboard, and the longer I had to wait, the more I could feel eyes drilling holes in the back of my head. I could even hear my name, and whispers of some version of "Did you know Kara was coming back today?" I was half-tempted to turn myself around and yell, *Hey, everyone! Get a good look!* But right as I was considering it, hands actually on my wheels, Mr. David finished what he was doing and turned around.

"Oh, good morning, Kara! It's great to see you back!" I watched his eyes. They traveled down from my face to my legs and lingered there a few moments longer than was polite. His mouth pulled down in a little frown as he seemed to consider my chair, and he drew his eyes back up again and tilted his head to the side. Ah, the sympathetic head tilt Ana had warned me about. I wondered if this was going to be the way everyone looked at me now. "I don't know if you got the makeup work I sent you so you could stay caught up—"

"I got it," I said. "But I haven't had much of a chance to work on it yet. Things have been a little crazy."

He let out a laugh that was too quick and too loud. "Fair enough," he said. "Well, we're in the middle of reading *Pride and Prejudice.* Did you get a copy from the library? I have a copy you can borrow right now if you need one, and you'll . . ."

He kept talking, but I hadn't even cracked the book, so listening to him was pointless. Especially because the bell to start class rang, and, just like on my journey from the parking lot, I could feel every eye in the room on me.

"Where do I sit?" I cut him off. I didn't care about what chapter of the book we were on; I'd be lost anyway. I just wanted to know where I could go to get away from all these eyeballs and pretend to melt into the floor.

"You can take your normal seat," he said. "I didn't give it away while you were gone." He laughed at this little joke of his, and he didn't seem to understand why I wasn't laughing along with him. Or moving from my spot.

"Uh, Mr. David." It was Sarah Donovan, the girl sitting closest to Mr. David's desk. "How is she supposed to get over to her desk? There's not enough room."

"Yeah," said Baker, the guy next to Sarah. "And wouldn't it be easier to have her pull up to a table instead of trying to move into a desk?"

On one hand, I was grateful to Sarah and Baker for speaking up in my behalf so I didn't have to snark at Mr. David on my own. But on the other hand, who were they to speak for me? I didn't ask for their help, and they weren't my friends. They didn't visit me in the hospital. They didn't send a card. Who were they to try to jump in now? Especially when I was perfectly capable of giving Mr. David attitude on my own. It's not like my mouth was paralyzed.

I decided to ignore them, and I kept on staring at awful Mr. David, who was now clearly regretting his dumb joke and shifting from foot to foot.

"Uh. Good morning, everyone," he said to the entire class. "Get out your *Pride and Prejudice* books and spend a little time reading chapter ten silently. I'm going to get Kara caught up on what she missed while she was gone."

Baker snorted as he leaned over to pull his book out of his bag, and I couldn't help but smile.

"Okay, Kara," Mr. David said, in a loud whisper. "We're going to need to find you somewhere to sit since you aren't going to be able to sit at your normal desk anymore." I bristled at the word "normal" without even thinking about why. "Where can we put you?"

We both looked helplessly around the classroom, where,

of course, everyone was staring at us instead of reading, but there wasn't even a table or anything in the back I could roll up to and disappear behind.

"I'm going to have to call up to the office and see if they have an extra table they can set up as a desk for you. For now, why don't you use my desk instead?"

"You want me to sit at your desk?"

He looked uncomfortable at his own suggestion, but it really was the only thing we could do for right now, aside from balancing all my folders and books on my lap and just staying in the middle of the aisle. So, while everyone watched instead of reading Austen, I wheeled myself to the very front of the class and unpacked my things right there on Mr. David's teacher desk. Right in the perfect spot for absolutely everyone in class to gape at me from behind their books until the bell rang.

The rest of class was torture, especially with Mr. David frequently forgetting I was sitting at his desk and trying several times to sit down or get something and then turning around all awkwardly. Finally the bell rang, after what seemed like an entire school year, and I could make my escape.

On my way out of class, a couple of people walked up to me and said hi and that it was good to see me and that they were glad I was doing better after the accident and blah blah blah. I watched their faces the same way I watched Mr. David's. They avoided eye contact too much, their gaze traveled down to my legs, where it lingered as their minds tried to make sense of what they were looking at, then—*bam!*—the sympathetic head tilt. I could hardly even pay attention to them when they were speaking to me because all I wanted to do was leave. Escape the conversation, go home, pretend I had never met these people. Their sympathy was smother-ing. Suffocating. I wanted none of it.

Ana sure was right about that damn head tilt, but she didn't mention how mortifying it was to be stared at like one of those starving children infomercials. I could almost see the thought bubble above everyone's head. *Poor Kara, she's ruined forever. But thank God it wasn't me.*

The rest of the day was about the same. Some teachers had tables in their rooms, or had heard I was coming back and was in a wheelchair and thought, *Hey, maybe I need a new desk space,* and they were prepared. I did have the awk-ward "sit at my desk for now" again in math, but luckily that was a class I had with Jack, and he sat right in front of Ms. Wiles's desk, so he spent the whole period entertaining me with stupid faces whenever we made eye contact.

I was going to try to keep track of how many times I got "the look" from people, but I stopped counting when I real-ized that I was getting it from everyone.

CHAPTER 10

The school day really crawls by when you're on display, and by the time lunch rolled around, it felt like I'd lived a thousand miserable lives. Jack and Amanda ambushed me when I was leaving my fourth-period class and all the staring eyeballs behind, and while I should have been surprised to see the two of them waiting for me, I really wasn't. Jack usually had lunch in the activities room with the other Student Government officers and Amanda typically worked through lunch in the media studio, but today they volunteered to have lunch with me anywhere I wanted to go. My choice.

"Don't worry about me, you guys," I said. "I don't want you changing your normal lunch plans to accommodate me." I didn't mention that I was totally lunch-less now that I was also Curt-less. My last school year had been spent in Curt's orbit, so I wouldn't even know where to venture for lunch on my own.

"It's really no problem," Amanda said. "The media studio is so dark. A little light will do me some good."

I appreciated their efforts, I really did. But I'd been drowning in a sea of pity all day; I didn't want their pity hangout, too.

But, more than that, I needed to take this opportunity to find Curt.

I tried not to show it after the first couple of days in the hospital, but Curt's lack of contact had me confused and upset. He was my boyfriend for almost an entire year. I went to his water polo games. He picked me up from dance practice. I taught his little sister how to pirouette and what stretches would make her kicks go higher.

This complete silence from him gutted me almost as much as the accident had. And it was so unlike him, too. Curt was a lot of things, but I never thought he was a dick.

Since he still wasn't answering my calls or my texts, I needed to see him face-to-face and find out what was up. Why he was ignoring me like this when I needed him the most. He probably heard I was back at school, and he'd done an excellent job of making himself scarce so far. But he was always over by the pool at lunch, and he couldn't move the whole water polo team from their usual spot just to ignore me. Plus, he knew I hated confrontation. He was probably banking on me not wanting to talk to him in front of an audience.

What he didn't realize was that it wasn't just the feeling in my legs the accident took from me. It also killed any anxiety I had about having this conversation in public. YOLO, and all that.

I smiled and waved good-bye to Jack and Amanda, who

looked genuinely concerned about me, and I wheeled myself way over to the pool area.

Sure enough, there was Curt. Laughing and smiling with his friends, drinking a Gatorade. Not dead in a ditch, like I'd told myself he might be when he didn't answer my texts. Not mysteriously out of the country, like I'd tried to convince myself was the reason he didn't call back. My denial over his absence had been so powerful that I honestly convinced myself there must be something horrifically wrong with him, which had to be the only reason for him to straight up ignore me. But, nope. He was right here where I knew he would be, healthy and normal.

Which meant the only reason he didn't answer my calls or my texts was because he didn't want to.

So here I was, rolling along in my wheelchair, my life completely upside down, while he was standing in his same lunch spot and laughing with his buddies. Un-freaking-believable.

Ideally, I would've liked to hide out for a second and come up with a plan of attack before saying something to him, since it really helped me to have a script in my head before I had "a talk" with someone. I'd had all day to figure this out, but between trying to get settled in all my classes and trying to avoid all the stares, I never really got any further in my mental conversation than, *Dude, what the hell?* And, given my current state as school novelty, I couldn't really hide out anywhere and get my thoughts together.

I was going to have to just go in and do this thing.

Without letting myself think about it too much, I pushed myself over to Curt and his friends, who were gathered into a loose clump in their usual spot by the pool. As I approached them, I felt a quick flash of relief that I was in the chair and not walking. I didn't have to worry about my legs shaking with nerves.

"Curt," I said as soon as I was close enough to say his name without yelling. He and his friends had been so caught up in whatever they were doing that they didn't hear me or see me approaching.

He turned around when he heard his name, and I watched an entire range of emotions pass over his face in a matter of seconds. Recognition, surprise, confusion, sadness, pity, and finally . . . nothing. After all that, he arranged his face so he had this completely detached expression.

Like he didn't even know me.

"Oh, hey, Kara," he said. "What's up?"

Of all the different reactions I'd expected from him, complete and utter indifference was nowhere on the list.

I drew my eyebrows together. "I was sort of wondering the same thing."

He shot a quick look at his buddies, who weren't very pro at faking like they weren't being nosy. He stepped closer to me and lowered his voice, but still kept up the act of indifference. "What do you mean?"

"I've called you. I've texted you. You haven't answered."

Something flashed through his face again, but it was gone in a second. "Why would I?"

"Because I was in an accident. I was in the hospital." My voice was so small, and I wished I could have sounded stronger. But there was strength in just being there. I knew it. "Because I'm your girlfriend."

His mouth twitched, and I watched as he managed to look around me. Over my head. To the side of my face. Never at my eyes and never, never at my legs. "Kara, you're not my girlfriend. Not after how you treated me at Rob's party."

"What?"

His voice shook. "You think you can just talk to me the way you did and—?"

"Are you insane? What do you mean, 'talk to you the way I did'?"

"At Rob's party. You made a scene. You were awful to me in front of everyone. That's not . . . I thought it was pretty clear that it was over."

My memories of the accident were foggy, nothing but darkness, fear, and confusion that floated around in the back of my mind. But the things that happened before, everything that happened at the party, I remembered all that like it was yesterday. I remembered telling Curt how much I needed to talk to him, making that clear several times. I remembered him leaving me outside alone, and I remembered finding him back in the house, getting drunk with his buddies and Jenny Roy hanging on him like a coat.

We'd argued, sure. But it wasn't a scene. It was a disagreement.

Not a breakup.

"No, Curt. It wasn't clear." I couldn't help it—the volume of my voice rose and rose. People were looking, and I knew it, but I had almost a month of frustration, anger, and confusion boiling up inside me, and it started to pour out. "We had an argument, Curt. We didn't break up."

He kept looking anywhere but my legs, where my hands were spread out, gripping my knees with so much force that it probably would have hurt if they'd had any feeling. He avoided my eyes, avoided everything about me, like, after almost a year of being my boyfriend, he couldn't even be bothered with me right now. "Yes, we did, Kara. How could I be with you after . . . after you made that kind of scene in front of everyone?"

The impact of his words was like another accident. Another reckless driver hitting me at full speed, sending me crashing through the windshield.

"You are so full of crap, Curt." I wasn't even trying to control the volume of my voice anymore, and his water polo buddies weren't at all trying not to stare. In fact, a small crowd may have gathered. "I'm your girlfriend, and I almost *died*. Did you even know that? Do you know that I'm paralyzed? A whole year together, and I can't believe that you—"

"Kara."

It was a voice that came out of nowhere, out of place in this situation, with these people, but also so, so familiar. And it was here to help me.

"Amanda, you need to handle your girl." Rob Chang spoke up from the middle of the crowd surrounding Curt. "She's getting a little angry."

"Maybe because your *boy* is being a complete dick to her." Amanda's voice was quiet, as usual, but it was strong, and she came around from behind me and squatted in front of my chair. "Let's go, Kara," she said. "They aren't worth it."

I opened my mouth to protest. *Of course Curt is worth it*, I was ready to say. *He's my boyfriend of almost a year. We've done everything together.*

But as I started to say something, I looked at him. And again, for a second something flashed in his eyes. Concern. Sadness. Maybe a little shame. Before I could really identify it, though, his eyes hardened and he turned back to his friends. Away from me.

"You're right," I said to Amanda, who, still squatting, had her hands resting on the arms of my chair like it was no big deal. "He's not worth it."

CHAPTER 11

Mom caught me staring out the window again. It wasn't like I was staring at anything in particular, like looking longingly out into the streets at the life I could have been having or anything emo like that. After my first week back at school, where I felt like I had to be "on" all the time, I was enjoying just zoning out. Home was the only place I could search for "going back to school in a wheelchair" on my phone and spend hours reading posts on disability message boards from people who were going through the same thing I was. It's where I could relax without people constantly asking me questions or treating me differently, where I didn't feel like I always had to be on my toes. Or whatever I would say now that I was never actually on my toes anymore.

At home, I could finally stop being "wheelchair girl" for a few hours, even if Mom was still tiptoeing around me and acting strange. At least she didn't stare like I was an alien from planet Feel Sorry for Me and ask dumb questions. But I found myself, during my downtime, not working on the huge pile of makeup homework or anything productive, but either Internetting on my cell or zoning out and staring out the window instead.

It seemed to be freaking Mom out.

"Kara," she said on Saturday morning, snapping me out of my latest trance. "I'm going to the grocery store. Do you want to come?"

Her words pulled me back to reality, but I didn't turn away from the window. Did I want to go to the store? Not really.

But should I get out of the house? Probably.

"I'm still in my pajamas," I said to the window.

"Well," Mom said in a voice of forced lightness. "That doesn't have to be a permanent condition, does it? You can always change."

I wanted to say, *No, I can't.* But she was just talking about my clothes and I wasn't, and I wasn't ready to have that conversation with her yet. And she wasn't ready, either, since she kept not talking about my legs and trying to act like everything was the same as it was a month ago.

"Come on, Kara." She sat in the chair at the table across from me. "It will do you some good to get out and do something normal."

There it was again, that word "normal." I was really starting to hate it.

I looked at the clock on the kitchen wall. Fifteen minutes to eleven. On any previous Saturday, I would have been putting on my dance clothes, getting ready to go to the studio for Saturday practice.

Suddenly I was hit with this overwhelming desire to be there. At the dance studio. I wanted to see my friends and watch them move across the floor. I wanted to listen to the music and close my eyes and pretend that I had a pair of legs that could still dance.

I finally looked at Mom. "Can we stop by the studio?"

At my mention of the studio, Mom's entire face lit up like Las Vegas. I was finally speaking her language again, and this was the first real smile I'd seen on her face since way before my accident. "Of course we can, sweetie." She reached over to put her hand on my knee, but I noticed her catch herself and move her hand to my arm instead. "I think that's a great idea. In fact, I can drop you off there while I do the shopping. That way you can take your time."

I caught my face before it completely fell and rearranged it into a halfhearted smile. I'd asked if *we* could stop by the studio. I wanted her to be there with me for this.

Mom didn't catch my disappointment, though, and she launched into gear. Fueled by the few shreds of my old life she managed to dig up, Mom pushed me to get showered, dressed, and into the car within half an hour. I didn't even have enough time to dwell on Mom distancing herself from me again or to think about the reality of what I'd decided. To really think about how seeing my dance friends would impact me.

That is, I didn't think about it until I was in front of the studio door, Mom having left me to go get groceries after telling me to "Give everyone my love!"

Once I was alone in front of the studio door, though, I thought about it. I thought about going in and watching everyone dance. How would that make me feel? At home, the idea had seemed comforting, but now, staring at the door of the studio, the familiar logo—a silhouette of a girl, leg high in an arabesque—on the window, comfort was the last thing I felt.

I was in the middle of considering how Mom would react if I just pushed myself over to the grocery store and met her there when the door of the studio swung open.

An unfamiliar woman came out the door. Tall and lithe, her hair was pulled back in a tight bun. A dancer. Probably looking for more information about classes for her daughter, or getting an application to be a teacher or something. She certainly didn't recognize me, either, because the look on her face when she saw me wasn't of pity or *Oh, poor Kara, look at what happened to you,* like the look I'd seen on the face of pretty much everyone I knew. It was only a look of surprise that I was lurking around outside the door.

"I'm sorry," she said. "Let me get this for you." She held the door open and smiled.

Until that moment, I'd been pretty sure I was going to go back to my mom at the store without going into the studio, but now this kind dancer woman who didn't give me the Look of Pity was holding the door for me and smiling and making me feel like I had to go in.

So I did.

The lobby of the studio looked like a generic office building. There was a small waiting area with stiff-backed chairs and a table scattered with outdated dance magazines. Susan, the owner's mom, was usually behind the receptionist desk, answering phone calls and making sure everyone had paid for and signed in for their classes. But on Saturdays, she was notorious for sneaking off to the Starbucks across the center for a latte once the classes were in session, and sometimes even popping into the nail place for a pedicure. That must be where she was now.

Without having to small-talk with Susan, which was one of the things keeping me from wanting to come inside in the first place, I could just wheel down the hall and watch the class—*my* class—for a while.

My Advanced Jazz class was in the second room, lovingly called "the Sauna," thanks to the faulty air-conditioning vent. We always complained about Sauna Saturdays, but with a couple of fans on hot days, it wasn't so bad. The heat kept our muscles loose, anyway.

The girls were still working on technique across the floor when I pushed myself up to the big window. I saw Christine, our teacher, clapping out a beat as the girls traveled from one side of the wooden floor to the other in a line, each one repeating the move they were practicing over and over again across the floor as Christine called out critiques of their form.

I didn't have to be able to hear Christine to know what she was saying about each girl. Sara had never been able to get her toes as pointed as they should be on her leaps. Amber's back leg looked like it was going to fly off into the sunset on its own. Paige's legs were perfect, but her hands always did a crooked thing that Christine could never seem to get her to correct.

I saw Christine say, "Paige! Hands!" as she clapped, and Paige stuck her tongue out the side of her mouth, biting down in concentration as she tried to make her hands look more natural. The whole scene made me laugh, and I felt washed up in a wave of nostalgia for a life that was mine less than a month ago.

Running technique wrapped up after a few minutes, and the class took a quick break before moving on. For the first time since I woke up in the hospital, I was glad to be in my chair. Because the window in the room was up so high, I knew that if anyone looked over in this direction, which they probably wouldn't, they would see only my head, and I could easily wheel myself back and get out of view in a hot second. I wasn't ready to get caught watching class. I wanted to go say hi on my own terms.

When I was ready.

After a quick break and some stretches, the girls got into a familiar formation. They were going to practice our lyrical routine for the fall recital.

I couldn't hear the music from the hallway, but I didn't need to. I knew every note by heart, just like I knew every move of this routine down to my bones. As the girls started to move across the floor, I found my hands absently moving along to the routine, as I would do anytime I heard this music out in the real world. I wasn't doing the arm movements full out or anything. My arms stayed right in the region of my lap, just following the flowy arm movements of the girls as they traveled across the floor with the music. But when they reached up an arm to the sky, my hand moved up to my face. They spread their arms open wide, and my hands followed suit.

Then came the big leap sequence. I'd been so lost in the music in my head and the moves my body knew without thinking, I didn't really register that it was coming up. But there they all were, leaping across the floor. And while I could follow along with my hands, I couldn't lift my foot to mimic their leaps. I couldn't make my body do what it naturally wanted to do. Dance with the girls, as I had my entire life.

I could feel the music in my soul, but I couldn't make my body follow along. My hands moved to the routine, but my feet remained in the footrests of my wheelchair, completely useless.

I knew I wouldn't be able to dance. The doctor told me that when I woke up in the hospital. And I knew I couldn't walk, obviously. But it was like all of that was being deflected by some kind of force field of denial in my mind. It didn't become hardened reality until this point, when I sat in the hallway of my dance studio, my home away from home for the past twelve years, and watched my friends dance this routine that I could do in my sleep while I was stuck in this chair with my useless legs.

I didn't even realize I was crying until the tears dripped into my mouth. I ran my entire hand over my face to wipe them away, but they kept streaming. And as soon as I realized how much I was crying, I started to panic a bit. I couldn't let anyone see me like this. I couldn't talk to any of these girls. What did I have to talk to them about, besides dance? What did we have in common if that was taken away? And how could I even fake casual conversation with these tears?

After wiping my wet hands on my jeans, I pushed myself back down the hallway as quickly as I could, praying that Susan was still at Starbucks so I wouldn't have to explain my sobbing as I hurried from the lobby. Thankfully, the receptionist desk was still empty. I wheeled myself around so I could back myself out the door without anyone knowing I was there, but right as I was about to push my chair into the door, it swung open.

Crap. Susan. I took a deep breath and tried to pull myself together for the small talk and pity party I was about to endure. But it wasn't Susan who said my name when the door swung open.

It was Jack.

"Oh, good," Jack said. "You *are* here." He let the door swing shut as he walked around my chair to see me, but he stopped short once he got a look at my face. "Oh my God, Kara. What happened? What's wrong?"

The look of genuine worry on his face made me lose any control I'd managed to gain over my whirlwind of emotions in the last few minutes, and the tears came again, fast and furious this time. I was ugly crying in the lobby of my former dance studio while my ex-boyfriend was looking on with equal parts concern and terror.

"Kara," he said over and over while I cried about the reality of never being able to dance again. "Kara, it's okay. It's okay." He kneeled down in front of me and leaned over, gathering me into a loose hug. "Whatever it is, it will be okay."

I wasn't usually a crier, and I couldn't think of a time I'd ever cried like this in front of Jack. Even our breakup was totally tear-free. Well, the part where I'd told him we shouldn't be together anymore was, anyway. Once he left my house, I'd curled up on my bed with Logan and sobbed into his fur. The breakup had been my decision, but that didn't mean it hadn't upset me.

After a few minutes of ugly crying into Jack's shoulder, I managed to get myself together before snot started running out of my nose without my knowledge. I used my palms to wipe my face again, and he hopped up and grabbed a box of tissues from Susan's desk.

"Here," he said. "Take all of these." He pulled tissue after tissue from the box and dropped them into my lap until all you could see was a mountain of white. I looked from his panicked expression to the pile of tissues on my lap and lost it. I just started laughing at how ridiculous this whole situation was, desperate and gasping laughs, and I couldn't stop for a good minute.

When I finally got myself together, I wiped off my face and asked him, "What are you doing here?"

"What?" He looked around as if he had forgotten where he was and what he was doing. "Oh. Oh, yeah! We're here to surprise you."

"You're . . . what?"

"Amanda and I stopped by your house to surprise you. But your dad said you were shopping with your mom. So we found her at the grocery store, but she said you were here. So now that we finally homed in on your location and this has become the most complicated surprise ever, we're kidnapping you. Your mom knows you're with us, so don't worry about her. You ready for this? You ready to get kidnapped?"

I don't know what was more surprising to me. That I was apparently being kidnapped, or that the two people I'd been pushing away the most before the accident were the ones who were going out of their way to be there for me now that I was Broken Kara. Tears sprang up in my eyes again, but this time I managed to control them.

Instead of giving in to the tears, I nodded. And I tried to smile, but I wasn't sure if it worked.

"Great," Jack said, and he was able to smile for real. "Amanda and I figured you could use a little fun after the week you've had. And it looks like we were totally right." He walked over to the door and held it open as I wheeled myself out, my lap still full of unused tissues.

As soon as we came through the door and into the parking lot, Amanda jumped out of the passenger seat of Jack's Civic. I watched as her face went from excitement to shock and confusion when she got a good look at Mount St. Tissue on my lap and my puffy cry face.

"Are you okay?" she asked, creeping slowly toward me. Like I might burst into tears again at any second if she crossed an invisible boundary.

I nodded. "I just had a moment in there. Watching everyone dance, and—"

"Well, it looks like we got here just in time, then, huh?" One thing I always liked about Amanda—she could really tell when there was something I didn't want to talk about, and she changed the subject immediately. I'd never realized what an important quality that was in a friend until this exact minute, because there was no way I could handle hashing this out without crying again.

"So, what are we doing?" I tried again to smile, and it felt much more convincing now than it had a minute ago in the studio lobby.

Amanda and Jack, who had now moved over to the car to open the back end to stow my chair, both smiled back at me. "We're taking you out to do some normal stuff," Jack said as he moved some boxes around in the back of the Civic. "Hope you're ready for an awesome day of normal."

Normal. That word again. But the way he said it didn't make me shudder.

Amanda picked up the big pile of tissues on my lap and gathered it into a ball, tossing it into the trash can outside the studio door. "You won't be needing these," she said. "Now, let's go."

"Thanks, guys. This sounds amazing."

And it really did. At that moment, nothing in the world could have possibly sounded better than normal.

CHAPTER 12

"So, where are we going?"

Jack pulled his Civic out of the parking lot once I'd gotten settled in the front seat. Using the meager contents of my purse and Jack's rearview mirror, I tried my best to get my face back in order after my sob sesh, but that didn't distract me from wondering where these two were taking me.

"What did we used to spend all of our Saturdays doing?" Amanda leaned forward from the backseat, her head popping out in the space between me and Jack, her eyes practically bulging out of her head with expectation.

"Well . . ." How *did* Amanda and I spend our time back when we were inseparable? It had been a while, honestly, since my weekends morphed into being dedicated to Curt and hanging out with his friends. "After I got home from the studio, we'd always go to the mall, and—"

"Bingo!" she said, smacking my arm playfully.

"We're going to the mall?" I arched my eyebrow in Jack's direction. "You hate the mall."

"Hey, now," he said, not taking his eyes off the road. "There is a lot of fun to be had at the mall."

"Yeah, for girls." I couldn't help but laugh at the image of Jack taking part in the Kara and Amanda Mall Crawl that used to happen every weekend.

"You need to stop it with your sexist propaganda, Kara Moore." Jack wagged his finger in my direction with a smile but quickly returned his hand to the wheel. "You're totally stereotyping me. I can be manly while having fun at the mall."

"Oh yeah?"

"Watch me."

"I can't wait for this," Amanda said, laughing and smacking Jack on the shoulder.

Ten minutes later we arrived in the mall parking lot. After a week of driving to school, we had all become experts at getting me and my chair in and out of the car, and the three of us arrived at the mall entrance within minutes.

But I hesitated outside the automatic mall doors, running my hands back and forth over my wheels without pushing them forward. It was sweet of Amanda and Jack to bring me here, but after a week of being stared at like a science experiment, a deep sense of dread pumped through my veins at the thought of having to go through it on the weekend, too. I had to go to school; I had no choice about that. But I didn't have to subject myself to stares here.

Jack must have sensed my trepidation, because he stopped and raised an eyebrow at me. "You okay?"

How could I explain the prickly feeling of wrongness

that erupted up and down my arms? The exhaustion of being the subject of nonstop stares? The sympathetic head tilt?

"Everyone looks at me," I said quietly.

"Don't flatter yourself," he said. "They're just staring at me. They can't keep their eyes off this. You know how it is." He took off his beanie, ran his hand through his tangled mess of blond curls, and winked.

I laughed at him, and the prickly feeling, the sense of dread, it eased just a little bit.

"You guys coming, or what?" Amanda yelled from between the automatic doors.

"Are we coming?" Jack asked me. His voice was soft and caring; he was really giving me a choice here.

I didn't want to disappoint him, not after everything he and Amanda had done to cheer me up. And I couldn't spend my life in my house. If people were going to stare, let them stare. I couldn't let them keep me from going out in public.

"We are," I said, pushing myself forward. "Let's do this."

"So," Jack said as the automatic mall doors shut behind us. "What's the first thing you girls would usually do on Mall Saturdays?"

Amanda and I shared a look and smiled. "Ice cream," we said in unison.

Jack laughed. "You thought ice cream was going to be too girly for me? It's like you don't know me at all. I thought you were going to say bra shopping or something." He shook his head. "And there are over eighteen hundred different flavors of ice cream, with many of them being extremely manly. Like bacon ice cream. That's downright masculine."

The first snag of the afternoon popped up when we followed our normal route to the food court and I realized that

I always took the escalator to get up there. In fact, Amanda had already stepped on it and was moving upward before she realized why we weren't behind her. "Oh, crap," she said. "I'm sorry, Kara. I didn't—"

"It's fine," I said. And it was. She really did look sorry as she started walking down the escalator that was trying its hardest to pull her up, but I laughed and waved her off. "Just go."

"We'll take the elevator," Jack said. "We'll meet you up there. Save us a seat or something."

"Where *is* the elevator?" I asked as we turned ourselves around.

"In the middle, I think?" He waved his hand absently toward the center of the mall. "I've actually never taken it. This will be an adventure."

The elevator was a bit of a journey from the escalator at the very end. "So many new things to get used to," I mumbled as we waited for the doors to slide open. "A million extra steps I have to go through now. It's ridiculous."

"It's not a big deal," Jack said as he tapped out a beat on the back of my chair. "It's good exercise. For both of us. Can you even imagine the arms you're going to have after just a few months of pushing yourself around? You're going to look incredible. Well, you already do, but you know . . ."

I blushed at his compliment, and I pushed myself through the doors as quickly as I could once they slid open. I didn't want him to get the wrong idea.

By the time we made it back across the mall to the food court, we found Amanda sitting at a table with a huge paper bowl from the ice cream place in the middle of it, three spoons sticking out the top.

"I cleared the chairs on that side of the table away so you could just roll right up." She waved her hand to the chair-free side of the table opposite her. She looked so proud of herself for thinking of it. It was nice she was trying to make up for the escalator incident, but I hoped that she wouldn't make such a big production of it every time.

"Thanks," I said as I scooted my chair under the table. "What's all this?"

"Well, I was going to get us each an ice cream, but they were having this deal for a banana split that had four scoops and you know what a sucker I am for a deal. But, sorry, Jack. No bacon."

One look at the huge banana split on the table in front of us sent my internal calorie counter spinning off the charts. It's not like I was obsessed with my weight or anything, but as a dancer, it's something I'd always been super aware of. And now that I couldn't dance, I couldn't really exercise as I always had. Pushing myself in my chair was obviously work ing my arms, like Jack said. Just like my dad had a running list of things he never thought about before, I guess I did, too. Would the rest of my body change with the loss of my legs?

But looking at the faces of my friends, I decided that would be something I could worry about tomorrow. Today, guilt-free banana split. Screw you, calories.

Once we finished the ice cream, Amanda laid out the plans for the rest of the day. "So, I was thinking, my favorite boss is working today, which means free movies for us. So movie first—"

"Come on! It's like you guys aren't even trying to make this hard on me," Jack broke in.

"—and then we can go try on shoes. Kara, your Toms are cute and all, but I think we should get something a little more fun on your feet. And I need to get some shoes for the Homecoming Dance." She paused. "I, uh, don't know if you're planning on—"

"Nope. Hell no. Not going." Homecoming posters had been popping up around school, and every one I saw was like a stab in the eyeballs. No Curt meant no date, which meant no Homecoming; I didn't want to be reminded of what I didn't have any more than I needed to be.

"But you can still try on some shoes, right? I mean, you still . . . ?"

At hardly over five feet tall, and dating a guy who was pushing six feet, I'd become obsessed with super-high heels in the past year. I didn't wear them to school or anything, but on dates with Curt, they had been awesome. They made my short legs look miles long, and they shortened the distance from my face to Curt's considerably. A pair of sky-high heels wouldn't keep me from feeling short anymore, but they could still be fun, right? And more than being fun, my heels might give me that boost of confidence they always brought to any outfit. They made me feel powerful and strong, like I could stand eye-to-eye and toe-to-toe with anyone.

But slip-on canvas shoes had been my staple since coming home from the hospital, just for ease and practicality. I wasn't even sure if I could wear those big ol' shoes anymore, to be honest. They were chunky and heavy, and I wouldn't be able to feel if they were staying on my feet or not. They might slide right off my foot and I wouldn't even know until I rolled over them with my chair.

I'd have to go home and do some research on this shoe situation.

"Yes, Amanda. I still like shoes." I poked Jack's arm with my plastic spoon. "So, can we find the sappiest romantic comedy ever, just to make sure Jack here gets the full experience?"

Jack shook his head. "As long as I don't have to try on heels later, I'm good."

"No, but you're helping us pick some out. You said you wanted the full experience." Amanda hopped up from her seat. "I'll go over to the theater to check the movie times and make sure my boss is cool with letting us in. Don't run off, okay?"

"I don't know," I said. "I was sort of planning on making a break for it."

"Har har," she said. "BRB."

I turned to Jack to ask him what movies were even out right now, since it was something I hadn't been paying attention to at all, but as soon as I saw him obsessively cleaning a small area of the table with a napkin, I knew something was up. Jack only got OCD when he was worried about something big.

"Uh-oh." I grabbed the napkin from his hand. "What's on your mind, Mr. Clean?"

"Um," Jack said, making eye contact for a second before looking past me. "There's something I need to tell you."

I crinkled my eyebrows. "About what?"

He blew air out of his pursed lips, and I felt like I could actually see the wheels turning in his head as he tried to figure out how to tell me whatever it was he was going to say.

"Just spit it out, Jack."

He made eye contact again and raised one side of his mouth into a tentative half smile. "You're still on the ballot for Homecoming Queen."

In the seconds before the words came out of his mouth, my mind sped through the different possibilities of what he might have to tell me. Out of everything that flashed through my mind, from terrible news about his parents to him coming out of the closet or something else totally out of left field, this was not something I even considered.

I blinked at him. "What?"

"I figured you didn't know," he mumbled. He cleared his throat and shifted painfully in his seat, like he was sitting on a knife. "In Student Government yesterday, we were reading through all of the nominations from each club to see who still needed to turn in a name, and I saw you were still listed there for water polo." He searched my face for a reaction, but I don't know what he saw there. My mind was racing.

"I guess I just assumed . . . ," I assumed that since Curt broke up with me and publicly humiliated me that he didn't want me representing his team. I figured that no one wanted a Homecoming Queen in a wheelchair. I guessed that since no one at school could actually look me in the eye that they would've taken my name off the ballot the second they heard about my accident.

I guess not.

"Do you think they forgot, or . . . ?" I trailed off because I didn't even mean to say it out loud.

Jack shrugged. "I guess they wanted to leave you on there. Although after the way those guys treated you . . ." I couldn't help but notice a sharp edge in his voice when he said that, and I knew that by "those guys" he meant Curt. "Anyway, I wanted to let you know because I wasn't sure if that's something you want or not."

"Thanks for telling me." I chewed on the tip of my thumb and stared off into the distance. "Of course I don't want that. Everyone would probably think it's some kind of joke or something. They all stare at me enough as it is. I don't need to give them more of a reason."

"People are only staring because they're curious, Kara. And they feel bad for you."

"I'm sick of people feeling bad for me." I grabbed a napkin from the table and started shredding it to pieces.

Jack leaned across the table and lowered his voice to almost a whisper. "They feel bad for you because they know how easily it could've been them. You shattered their 'it won't happen to me' illusion. That blows their minds, so they stare. But once they get through their head that this is how it is now, they'll stop staring. Things will go back to normal."

"For them," I said, anger creeping into my voice. "But not for me. I'll never walk again. I'll never dance again. I'll be in this chair while they forget about what happened and go back to thinking that it won't happen to them. Which it won't. But it did happen to me." Hot tears pricked up in my eyes, and I bit down hard to keep them from falling. I hadn't admitted this to anyone. I'd barely admitted it to myself.

I watched Jack's face register what I'd said and the tears gathering in my eyes. His eyes crinkled and the sides of his mouth turned down. He moved his hand from the back of my chair to my knee, and he squeezed it. I couldn't feel it, obviously, but I watched him do it, and it wasn't lost on me that he was the first person besides the doctors to actually

touch my legs. Everyone else avoided them like they had actually been chopped off my body and I was wheeling myself
around on my chair with bloody stumps.

"I wish I could make things go back to the way they were
for you, Kara. I really do." His voice caught and he moved
his hand quickly from my leg. "So does Amanda." He cleared
his throat and stood up. "You know we're here for you. Both
of us. For whatever you need."

"I know. Thank you."

"I really do think you should go through with it, though.
The Homecoming thing. I think it would help you feel like
yourself again."

I shook my head. "That's not who I was before the accident, anyway."

"Yeah. But I know you feel like everyone is looking at you.
This way they would be looking at you on your own terms,
you know? They're looking because you want them to look."

He had a point. If people were going to stare, it might as
well be because I put myself out there. But still, ugh. No.

"And I need to come up with a ridiculous fund-raiser.
There's no way I'm doing that." There was a fund-raising
element to our Homecoming that allegedly started out as a
way to make the whole thing more than just a popularity
contest. It was split up fifty–fifty: half of the queen selection
was done through voting for the candidate, and half was
done through voting by donating spare change to your favorite fund-raiser and seeing which raised the most money.
But the fund-raisers had all morphed into silly, frivolous
things, and it became an unspoken contest between all the
queen nominees to come up with the most ridiculous project.
A few years ago, someone raised money to pay for the princi-

pal to buy some more fashionable clothes, and last year the girl who won raised money to buy a star and name it after our school mascot.

And it wasn't just that. I was sure water polo didn't want me, and after the way Curt and all those guys treated me, I wanted nothing to do with them.

"Listen, it's your decision," Jack said. "But I think you putting yourself out there will be a reminder for people. They can't forget it could happen to them if you keep reminding them, you know? So, will you think about it?"

He was right —I couldn't change what had happened to me, but maybe I could be a reality check for other people. Plus, part of me didn't want to give up on that crazy dream of being Homecoming Queen, and another part of me didn't want Curt to think he could treat me the way he did and get away with it.

But my plan at school was to blend in. Become invisible and hide myself from the sympathetic head tilt, not put myself right in the path of it.

"I'll think about it," I said. "That's all I can promise right now."

"Kara, you can do this. You can do anything." Jack looked at me like he actually believed this, and it made me feel the most normal I had in weeks.

I reached for his hand and squeezed his fingers. I opened my mouth to thank him. For his belief in me and his encouragement. For being so supportive and making me feel like myself. But I didn't get a chance.

"Did you guys miss me?" Amanda bounded back across the food court, almost slamming into Jack. "The mushiest romance ever is about to start in twenty minutes, and my boss is happy to let us in free. Let's go, team."

But my mind was a million miles away from the movie. Instead, I was replaying my conversation with Jack over and over.

Could I do this?

Could Wheelchair Girl actually run for Homecoming Queen?

CHAPTER 13

On our way home from the mall, Amanda leaned from the backseat into the space between me and Jack. "Can you take me home first? I'm not feeling well. Too much popcorn, I think."

"Sure," Jack said. "I'll drop you off real quick and then I'll take Kara home."

"Well, that's dumb." I twisted around to look at Amanda, who was clutching her stomach. "There's no point in dropping you off and then making him take me home when you guys live right next door to each other."

"I really don't feel well, Kara," she said, and I guess she did look a little green. "I'd rather be home, like, now. You don't mind, right, Jack?"

Jack shook his head. "It's not that far. I don't mind."

So, even though it made no sense, Jack dropped Amanda off, drove past his own house, and took me home.

"You should come in," I said as he unloaded my chair from the back of his car. "Mom would love to see you."

But Mom was too busy making dinner to say much more than hi when Jack walked behind me into the kitchen, and Dad was zoning out in front of the TV to a documentary about dogs who go to war while Logan snoozed in his lap.

"Uh." I had no idea what to do with Jack now that he was in my house, but telling him to just leave seemed rude. "Want to hang out for a bit? You can see my new room. Although, spoiler alert, it looks exactly the same as the old one."

Jack stared at me for a second with this strange look on his face, like I'd asked him if he would like to snuggle with my pet porcupine or something. "You want me to hang out? With you? At your house?"

He was right; it was a little unusual. We hadn't hung out just the two of us since we broke up. But he was here, and we'd had a really fun day. Why not?

I shrugged. "Yeah. I mean, if you want to."

He blinked at me a couple of times before shaking himself out of whatever daze he seemed to be in. "Of course I want to," he said, smiling. "Lead the way."

I yelled to my parents that we would be in my bedroom if they needed us, and I led him down the hallway to my new room.

Back when Jack used to come up to my bedroom all the time, back when we were together, my parents made a point to say, "Leave the door open!" anytime we headed up the stairs. I was a lot younger then, and Jack and I knew better than to make out in my house when they were home, so we were mostly doing homework or playing video games. But my parents would still walk by my room often, popping in with snacks for us or urgent questions that couldn't wait another second.

And the only time Curt was allowed in my bedroom was when my parents weren't home and didn't know he was there, so "allowed" wasn't exactly the right word.

But this time when Jack and I went into my room, my parents didn't say a word.

"Close the door," I said to Jack as soon as we were both in my new bedroom.

"Okay." He eased the door shut behind him, and I could tell from his tone that he thought I was about to share some big, secret news with him when really I just wanted to see how my parents would react to having a boy in my room with the door closed.

Was it that clear to them that Jack and I weren't going to do anything? It should have at least crossed their minds that I was going to be alone in a room with a guy I'd once rounded the bases with. Did they just assume I was damaged goods now and they didn't think of me as a teenage girl who might be after a little action? It wasn't that difficult to believe that Jack could still think about me that way.

Or maybe they were so busy trying to ignore each other that they were ignoring me, too.

I lifted myself out of my chair and plopped onto my bed, scooting and adjusting myself back against the line of pillows against the wall. Jack moved forward like he was going to help me, but he seemed to decide against it at the last second and instead pushed my chair up to the wall. After I was settled, he clicked through the playlists on my computer, finally selecting one and pressing Play, and he plopped down and arranged himself in the hot pink beanbag chair across from me.

As soon as the first few notes came out of the speakers, I recognized his song choice. This was the first song on a playlist of mellow songs he'd made for me back during freshman year. I didn't have too much time to wonder what his music choice meant, or if it even had a meaning, because he started talking almost immediately, making plans for picking me up for school on Monday morning and talking about making posters or something for Student Government before first period. I knew I should pay attention, but my mind kept wandering to the song that was playing. He made this playlist for our first Homecoming Dance together, when we sneaked out of the dance early and he made me a picnic on the grass outside the Science classrooms. We listened to music and I taught him how to do a pirouette and we drank sparkling cider and kissed under the stars. It was one of my favorite memories of our time as boyfriend and girlfriend, and I hadn't thought of it in months. I wondered if it was one of his favorite memories, too.

I snapped back into reality when Jack leaned forward on the beanbag chair, resting his arms on his knees. "What else can I do for you, Kara? What do you want?"

I stared at the tendrils of hair curling up under the edges of his beanie, and I wondered why he was being so nice and doing so many things for me. I broke up with him over a year ago, and he'd been trying so hard to stay in my life when I wanted nothing more than to move on. And now that I was broken, he was back in my life like he'd never left. Why? What was he getting out of this?

"I think you should go home." It wasn't what I'd meant to say, and I don't even know where it came from. But once the words were out of my mouth, I was surprised by how true they were. I didn't want him to feel like he *had* to be here. I didn't want his pity. I was getting it from everyone else; I couldn't handle it from him, too.

Jack recoiled like I'd slapped him. "Um, okay," he said, lifting himself up from the beanbag chair. "I guess I'll see you Monday morning, then."

"Wait, Jack." I reached out my hand in his direction as he walked to the door. My hand didn't quite reach him, so I leaned over an inch or two so my fingers grazed his arm. "That's not what I meant. I just mean, I don't want you to— why are you doing this? Why are you spending so much time with me? And helping me? We're not . . ."

I didn't let myself say "we're not together anymore," which was what I was thinking. But I didn't know what to say instead, so my words just trailed off into silence as he stared at the door of my bedroom.

"You know what I really want?" I said after a long moment. "I want to be able to dance again. I want to walk. I want my legs to work. That's what I want."

Jack sighed. He stepped back from the door and sat down next to me on the bed. "You will, Kara. I know you will."

"You don't know that."

"Yes, I do. Because you have always gotten everything you wanted. You've gotten things you didn't even know you wanted. That's just the kind of person you are."

My nose crinkled. "Way to make me sound spoiled."

"Not spoiled." He smiled. "Charmed. There's a difference."

I snorted, and then I laughed because I totally didn't mean to snort. "I think you have me confused with someone who is not paralyzed and in a wheelchair. Newsflash: There's nothing charmed about my situation."

"Isn't there?" he said, tilting his head to the side. "You'd rather be dead?"

"No, but—"

He adjusted his beanie. "You need to turn your attitude around, okay? You could have died and you didn't. You have a life you could have lost. That's awesome."

"But I lost the thing I love the most. I can't dance anymore. I'm not—"

. He put up his hand. "Stop it, okay? Stop talking about yourself like you're ruined. You know, there's a whole segment of people with spinal cord injuries who—"

This time I cut him off. "Why do you do that?"

"What?"

"The random facts. The trivia and the inspirational quotes and all that. You never used to do that before."

He stared down at his hands, fingers spread out on his knees, and a little pink flushed his cheeks. After a too-long silence, he looked back at me and shrugged. "I missed you, okay? I know you moved on and had your Ken doll boyfriend, but I missed having you in my life and I wanted a way to be your friend again. I know it's dumb, but it was all I could think of."

His words sent a flutter through me. An unfamiliar flutter that started in my stomach and spread all the way to my fingers, warming me from the inside out.

"You looked up all that random crap just for an excuse to talk to me again?" It was so Jack to go to all the trouble of thinking up an elaborate excuse to text me when any other person would have been fine with "Hi!"

He laughed. "Hey, I learned a lot. It was very educational."

"Well, you can stop it now, okay? We're friends again, so you don't have to think up cheesy things to say to me."

"You don't like the fun facts?"

I locked eyes with him. "They aren't you, Jack."

Memories of my relationship with Jack filled my mind. Jack and I holding hands as we walked into school together on our first day of freshman year. Jack and I throwing tennis balls for Logan at the dog park, challenging each other to quote movie trivia with each ball Logan brought back to us. Jack in the audience of every one of my dance recitals, always waiting for me after with flowers. *That* was Jack.

"Yeah," he said. "You're right. But it worked, didn't it? We're friends again."

"I guess."

"Well, as your friend, I feel it's my duty to remind you that you aren't ruined. You're different. Kara 2.0. And maybe Kara 2.0 should try some things that Kara 1.0 would never have done."

I knew when he said that, he was talking about Homecoming. Putting myself out there in front of the entire school, wheelchair and all. I don't know why me running for Homecoming Queen was so important to him. It's the kind of thing we would have laughed at back in the day. But maybe there was more to it than just Homecoming.

"I'll think about it," I said, chewing on the tip of my thumb. Before I could stop it, a huge yawn came out of nowhere, and I slapped my hand over my mouth in an effort to hide it.

"You're tired," he said, getting up from the bed and fighting back a yawn himself. "I should go home. But think about what I said earlier, okay?"

I rolled my eyes and smiled. "Thank you, Jack."

"See you Monday." He leaned forward, wrapping me up in a tight hug. And as he pulled back, he stopped and pressed a quick kiss onto my cheek.

It was an innocent kiss on the cheek from an old, good friend, but it left me stunned. And I felt it burning on my skin long after Jack had gone home.

Even though we'd talked about so much more, Jack saying "You'd rather be dead?" stayed in the back of my mind all night.

I had survived the accident, but the guy who hit me, the drunk driver, hadn't. I asked some questions about him and the logistics of what happened right after I woke up in the hospital, but Dad was quick to tell me not to focus on it, to put my energy into recovery instead. And when I asked Mom for any details, she changed the subject as quickly as she could. Even Amanda and Jack had warned me not to look into it, saying the whole thing would just upset me. So, since I couldn't remember the accident anyway, and adjusting to my future in a wheelchair was more than enough for my brain to process, especially with all the meds I was on, I put it out of my mind.

But that night as I tried to fall asleep, Jack's mention of how easily I could have died triggered something in my head. And his comment coupled with the morbid curiosity that comes alive in the middle of the night prompted me to do a search for my accident and see what came up. I typed "Kara Moore + accident" into the search on my phone and chewed on my thumb while I waited for the results to load.

At first, I couldn't understand what I was looking at; the picture that loaded on my phone screen didn't make any sense at all. It wasn't until I enlarged it that I was able to see that the unrecognizable blob I stared at was my car. My poor

Prius, a gift from my parents on my sixteenth birthday, crumpled into an indecipherable pile of metal bits and pieces.

I was in there, I thought as I stared at the horrific photo. My mind struggled to reconcile that fact with the image on my screen, so I kept thinking it over and over. *I was in there. I was in there.*

Eventually I made myself move on from the photo, and I scanned the attached article for any piece of new information until I found what I was looking for. The name of the driver.

Kyle Hayes.

Kyle Hayes was twenty-nine years old, single, and had two previous DUIs and a suspended license. He'd been kicked out of a bar earlier in the night—probably around the time I had been sitting out on Rob Chang's patio waiting for Curt— for being too drunk, but someone put him in a cab. It's unclear how he ended up behind the wheel of his car that night, the police said.

And now he's not around to ask.

There was a small photo of him at the bottom of the article, and seeing the face of the man who had changed my life was more of a stab in the chest than seeing my shredded car. I guess I'd been expecting the guy who drunk-drove his car through a red light and right into my spine to look trashy and gross, like some pathetic loser who didn't have a handle on his life. Like someone who lurked in back alleys and wore dirty tank tops and smelled like cigarettes and failure. But he didn't. Kyle Hayes had worked in pharmaceutical sales, the article said, and he was actually sort of hot.

I guess even hot guys can get drunk and ruin someone's life.

I couldn't get comfortable as I tried to fall asleep, and no amount of turning over from my front to my back and over again was helping to clear Kyle Hayes and my broken car from my mind. I still couldn't process what I had seen of the accident, but looking up that article did prove one thing to me: Jack was right. I was lucky to be alive. Charmed.

A second chance at life, that's what I had in front of me. Now all Kara 2.0 had to do was figure out how to use it.

CHAPTER 14

Missing homework was avalanching in a big way, so Monday morning I got to school early to stop in to a few classes and beg for some forgiveness. First stop was English with Mr. David, who needed to give me a makeup quiz on the beginning of *Pride and Prejudice*.

"Ah, good morning, Kara," he said when he saw me lurking in his doorway. "Come on in. I have your quiz right here."

Luckily, the quiz was pretty easy, thanks to SparkNotes and Colin Firth, and I finished in a matter of minutes. I had tried to read the chapters, really I had, but all the meds the doctors had me on left me staring at the book without registering a single word. "Is there anything else I need to make up while I'm here?"

"Oh, I'm sure there is," he said, and clicked away on his computer, probably checking out my grade. "You sure have a lot to catch up on, don't you? That must be tough on you. With everything you're going through and all."

"Yeah, between making up homework, physical therapy, and—" I took a deep breath and prepared to say it out loud. "—now starting my fund-raising campaign for Homecoming, it's going to be a lot to do. But I can handle it." I let a smile creep into my voice as I said the words, thinking back to my talk on Saturday with Jack. After spending all Sunday deliberating, I'd decided he was right. I could do this and I should do this. I deserved to do something to get my life back to normal. I shouldn't let Kyle Hayes continue to have power over me.

Mr. David's head snapped up from his computer at my mention of Homecoming, and he tilted his head and crinkled his eyebrows. "You're in the running for Homecoming Queen?"

I nodded. "Water polo nominated me before the accident."

"Oh," he said. "Have you talked to them since then? I mean, now that you're . . . ?"

Did he seriously just say that? Of course he did—he's a jerk.

I opened my mouth to reply, but he kept on yammering.

"You know, they might not even realize . . . you should probably go over to Activities after this and talk to Mrs. Mendoza."

"What are you saying?" I'd always gone out of my way to be extra polite to teachers, but no teacher had ever made me feel as small and worthless as Mr. David just had. No *person* had, actually, and his words exploded like shrapnel in my head, causing more damage the longer they bounced around in there.

And, the funny thing was, I didn't even care about Homecoming all that much. When Jack told me my name was still on the ballot, my first instinct was to roll in to school as fast as my wheels would take me and ask to be taken off. But Jack's belief in me sparked something, a desire to push myself out of my comfort zone. And after reading about my accident, I'd poked around some of the disability message boards I spent my nights reading, and I learned that there were lots of girls in wheelchairs around the country doing awesome things at their schools.

I'd started to think that maybe this whole thing could be fun.

I guess not.

Mr. David stood up and walked toward me. "Don't get me wrong, Kara. I was only saying—"

Hands shaking, I gripped my wheels and rolled myself back. Away from him. "You were only saying that water polo wouldn't want some cripple representing them at Homecoming. Just that a girl in wheelchair would never win anyway, so why bother. Right? That's what you were saying?"

"Kara, no. That's not—"

"That's sure what it sounded like to me." The classroom felt like it was closing in on me, and I wanted desperately to get out of there. But another disadvantage of a wheelchair is that you can't really make a dramatic exit. There's no wheelchair equivalent to "turning on your heel and storming out." I pretty much had to maneuver a three-point turn to get myself toward the door again, but once I was facing the right way, I pushed myself out of that classroom as fast as my arms could manage. Mr. David called after me the whole time, but I ignored him.

I couldn't ignore what he'd said, though.

In all honesty, he put in words exactly what had been running through my mind since I started back at school. I wasn't a normal girl anymore, not a girl who could win Homecoming. I was Wheelchair Girl now, and no one would vote for Wheelchair Girl. I was sure water polo didn't want me.

But I wasn't going to let Mr. David get to me, was I? He was a jerk to everyone, all the time. No one ever believed the completely insensitive and insulting things he said. Why should I start now?

Stopping at the corner, I ran my hands through my hair over and over as Mr. David's words repeated in my head. Somewhere in there, my conversation with Jack was trying to break through—but Mr. David's words were louder. They resonated so loudly because they were an echo of my own thoughts.

I pushed myself forward, in the direction of the activities room. Of course, the first person I saw when I got there was Jack, making his Red Ribbon Week posters outside the door with some of the other Student Government people. "Hey, Kara!" All smiles, he hopped up from his poster making and came over to me. "Are you going in? Allow me." He held open the door and followed me inside. "Did you come here to help with posters or something? Did you get my mental signal that we're short on girls with nice handwriting this morning? No one should let me write the posters. I thought they learned that from the prom debacle last year."

"I'm actually looking for Mrs. Mendoza. Is she here?"

The problem with someone like Jack, whom I've known so well for so long, is that he knew all my voices. My happy voice, my scared voice, my nervous voice, my fake voice. So I

couldn't even pretend like I was there for some innocent reason. He could hear it in my voice.

"Kara, no."

"I just . . . I can't do it." I let out a long sigh and told him
about the conversation I'd had with Mr. David.

Jack's face grew redder and redder as I filled him in. "How
does this guy still have a job? My God," he said as he clenched
and unclenched his fists. "That's not true, Kara. You know
it's not true."

But before I had a chance to reply, Mrs. Mendoza walked
into the room, holding a coffee mug the size of her head.
"Oh, good morning, Kara. Nice to see you." I watched as her
eyes darted from my face, down to my legs, and back to my
face again, wrapping up with the head tilt. Like, did people
think my legs would have disappeared? Or they would be all
shriveled up? Or I would suddenly stand up and tap dance? I
don't know what they expected, but they always looked.

"I think I'm going to take my name off the nomination
list for Homecoming." I'd been hoping my voice would sound
decisive and commanding, but instead it shook and came out
at almost a whisper.

"You are?" She put down her coffee and leaned over the
counter that separated us, resting on her elbows and looking
at me with concern. "Why?"

"She's not," Jack said, and he actually grabbed the back of
my chair and started to push me away. "She's kidding. Very
funny, Kara. Let's go."

"Don't you dare," I said through gritted teeth. "Move me
back."

He righted my chair and let out a defeated sigh. "Fine,"
he said. "I'll be outside."

"Are you sure about this, Kara?" Mrs. Mendoza said after Jack went back outside to continue his posters.

I nodded. "I'm sure water polo is just leaving me on the ballot to be nice." Nice wasn't the word I'd use to describe my last encounter with the water polo team, but Mrs. Mendoza didn't need to know that. "They nominated me before the accident because I was Curt Mitchell's girlfriend. But Curt and I aren't together anymore, and I think they feel bad taking me off." This was way too much information to share with a teacher, but for some reason I couldn't stop talking.

"Okay, if you insist." Mrs. Mendoza picked up a clipboard from her desk. "I'm sure they left you on the list because they wanted you representing them—"

"More likely they just forgot." I let out a humorless laugh that sounded more like a snort.

She took a big sip from her coffee. "So, I'm going to take you off the list as water polo's nominee and let them know they need to pick someone new. And you'll be officially out of the running for Homecoming Queen." She narrowed her eyes at me. "Are you sure that's what you want?"

I remembered the feeling of excitement that flooded me back when Curt told me I was their nominee. Homecoming was something I'd always secretly hoped for and never thought would actually happen. Since it was a ridiculous dream to begin with, it wasn't so hard to give it up now.

"I'm sure," I said with as much conviction as I could muster.

I flinched as she crossed out my name.

That was it. The last of Old Kara, gone. Kara who was a dancer and who had a boyfriend and who had a chance of being Homecoming Queen and having a normal senior year and a normal life. That Kara was finally eliminated with one drunk driver to the side of the car and one firm stroke of ballpoint pen across what was left.

Jack waited for me outside the activities room, and when I came through the door, he was angry. I could tell by the wrinkle between his eyes.

But I was angry, too.

"How dare you try to move me without my permission, Jack. Don't you ever do that to me again."

"I'm sorry about that, Kara. I really am." He let out a sigh. "But I didn't want to see you make a mistake."

"Taking my name off the ballot isn't a mistake. It's my choice. Just like where I want to be and where I want to go is my choice. Not yours."

He stared at his Converse for a few seconds before he looked back up at me, his face hardened. "You know they're just going to nominate Jenny Roy in your place." He pretty much spat her name out.

I rolled my eyes. I was in no mood for his drama. "I told you at the mall that I didn't really want to do it. I let you talk me into thinking that I could be normal, that this would all be normal. But we both know it won't be, Jack, and I don't want to pretend that it will. Even as Kara 2.0, I'm not Homecoming material. Everyone knows that."

"God, Kara, it's not like you're damaged goods. And I know you. There's no way you're okay with just handing Jenny Roy something that should be yours."

"Actually, it's perfect," I said bitterly. "Now everyone gets what they want, right? Water polo doesn't have to regret nominating me or feel guilty for taking me off, Jenny Roy gets her moment of Homecoming glory, and I get to not get stared at and humiliated in front of the whole school. Win—win—win."

"Kara, you know—"

"Just leave it, okay, Jack? I've obviously disappointed you, but this is how it is. Awful Mr. David is right for once. I have no business being on Homecoming Court. I don't want everyone's pity, and I'd rather just let it go. Can you respect that? Please?"

Jack blinked a few times and pulled his lips tight into a line. He let out a long breath and said, "Fine. I'm sorry." I didn't see what he did after that, because the bell rang, so I turned myself around and pushed on to my first class with one less thing on my mind. Now I could go back to trying my hardest to disappear into the crowd.

CHAPTER 15

In an effort to fake some normalcy and family togetherness, Mom and I spent most evenings on the couch. We watched trashy reality TV with Logan curled up between us while I worked on my homework and looked at videos on the Internet until Dad got home and pretended that everything was exactly as it should be. Tonight I was boycotting Mr. David's *Pride and Prejudice* homework out of spite; Mom and I were both quiet, staring at the screen while Logan snored away. None of us had expected the doorbell, and when it rang, Logan let out two enthusiastic barks, Mom's head swung toward me, and she opened her mouth for just a second but closed it quickly.

"You were going to ask me to get it, weren't you?" It was supposed to be a joke, and I tried to smile at my mom. I mean, sometimes I forgot I wasn't the only one who had to adjust to the independence that I'd lost with my legs. Sure, I could get the door, but Mom would have to get up and pull my chair closer so I could scoot myself into it. By the time I got in my chair and got over there, the people at the door would probably start getting impatient, and it would be way easier for Mom to just get the door herself. So, I tried to make a joke about it. But I could tell as I looked at her reaction that my tone was all wrong and my face was all wrong and that somehow my joke and my smile got messed up somewhere between my head and my mouth.

Mom pushed herself up from the couch and didn't look at me. "Of course not, Kara."

From the entryway, I could hear a muffled "Surprise!" and Mom laughing, and a few seconds later she returned to the TV room with Jack and Amanda, who was carrying a huge pizza box. Logan, who had jumped off the couch with Mom, was trailing close behind the food, tail wagging enthusiastically.

"Look who stopped by for dinner," Mom said in a fake-cheery voice. "Now I can tell your father not to rush home." Her voice strained when she mentioned my dad, and I wondered how much had been going on behind the scenes between the two of them lately. The blankets were still folded by the couch, but if the two of them were still fighting, at least they weren't doing it in front of me anymore.

"We figured you could use some dinner," Amanda said. She disappeared into the kitchen with the pizza, and Mom followed behind her, offering to help.

"Hey," Jack said. He lurked in the entrance to the TV room, shifting from one foot to the other. Speaking of strained, things had been bumpy between us since the Homecoming debacle, and I hadn't made too much of an effort to ease the bumpiness. I wondered if him showing up out of the blue like this was some sort of peace offering.

"Hey," I said. "Why don't you sit down instead of standing there all awkward? We're watching trashy reality TV."

Jack smiled. I guess I'd said the right thing, because the awkwardness melted off of him. Well, the extra awkwardness, anyway.

He settled into the couch next to me. "So, what terrible show is this?"

I patted the empty space between us, and Logan hopped up, stepped over a stray pillow, and curled himself up in my lap. I scratched the soft fur between his ears. "This dude is looking for love, and all of the girls are wearing masks and fat suits, so he has to judge them based on personality."

"Are you serious? This can't really be a thing."

"I swear. It's so ridiculous, but we can't look away. It's like a—" I'd almost said it was like a car wreck. That was a saying I should probably weed out of my vocabulary.

I caught Jack up on the events of the awful reality show as Amanda and Mom came back in the room with plates of pizza and glasses of soda. We finished the dumb show and started another one, and we laughed and talked and for a little bit I even forgot about my legs because I was sitting on the couch eating pizza with my friends and my mom and my dog, just like before the accident.

I should have known it wouldn't last long.

"So, Amanda, how is everything going with your video production class?" Mom had always been interested in Amanda's video stuff. And Jack's involvement in Student Government and leadership. And, of course, Dance Mom-ing me like she was the one up onstage.

"Oh, it's great!" Amanda launched into a rundown of her latest video projects as I ate my pizza and zoned out. I was pretty interested in Amanda's videos, but she'd filled me in on what she was up to at the mall on Saturday, so I didn't need to hear it all again.

"That sounds fascinating," Mom said while Jack and I rolled our eyes at each other. "What will you be working on next?"

"Well—" She wiped the pizza grease off her face with her napkin and kept on talking. She always got so into her projects. "—my media teacher is pushing me to enter this statewide video contest that has a big scholarship prize. It's all about teens being active and stuff, so he suggested I do something with the cross-country team at school." She let out a dramatic sigh as she leaned over and slid her empty pizza plate onto the table. "I don't know, though. I mean, I know nothing about running. I hate running. I wish I never even had to think about running."

I don't know what it was about her comment, but it hit me like a ton of bricks. Without even thinking, I snapped, "Well, at least you have the option to run if you want to."

She reacted as if I'd slapped her, and in a way I had. But she'd sort of slapped me, too, with her casual condemnation of something she took for granted and I so desperately wanted. To be honest, I'd always hated running, too. The happiest day ever was when I completed my PE credits after sophomore year and no longer had to run the dreaded mile at school. "I only run if someone is chasing me," I told people with a laugh when they told me they liked to run for fun.

But now that I *couldn't* run, not even if someone was chasing me, it seemed like a precious thing. I'd give anything to be able to whine about running again. And here she was complaining about it.

Amanda waved her hands around, like she was trying to shoo her comment out of the room. "Oh, Kara, I didn't mean—"

"Kara." Mom's voice was quiet, but the look in her eye was a warning. She lifted herself up from her place on the couch and busied herself clearing her plate, leaving me to deal with the tension that was growing by the second. I watched her as she retreated to the kitchen; then I turned to Jack, who looked like he was about to say something, too.

I felt cornered.

"Well, it's true," I said to Jack before he had a chance to join the pile on me. "It sucks to hear people complain all the time about walking too much or running or 'OMG, my feet hurt, I wish I could chop them off.' I mean, my God, do you know what I would give to have my feet hurt?"

"I'm *so* sorry, Kara," Amanda said. "I really didn't mean to—"

"I know you didn't mean to. You didn't even think about it, right? You didn't think about walking through the gate at school without me or going up the escalator at the mall. You never think about what you can do and I can't."

Jack still didn't say anything. He stared down at his knees, frowning. But Logan must have sensed the drama because he let out a low growl, hopped off my lap, and ran down the hall, probably to hide under my bed. I wished I could have gone with him, because I didn't even know where any of this was coming from. I hated confrontation, but I also hated how very different I was feeling lately—even though I was still completely myself, and how none of the people closest to me seemed to understand.

"Kara, that's not nice." Jack's voice was tight and quiet in the loudest of ways.

I knew in my heart he was right. I was being mean for no reason, and I should apologize to Amanda. But something about him, again, trying to tell me what I should say and how I should feel made me even more upset. Old Kara would have just walked away or stormed out of the room. But now, since I was stuck on the couch for the time being, I just lost it. I couldn't leave; I had all these people telling me what to do. I couldn't handle it anymore. "Amanda's the one who was being insensitive."

It wasn't what I meant to say. Not really. It was like words were pouring from my mouth and I couldn't adjust the faucet.

"You know what, Kara?" Amanda stood up. Her voice shook and her cheeks were flushed. "I have done nothing but be here for you since your accident."

"No one made you—"

"I know no one made me. But that's what friends do. I went to the hospital every day because you are my best friend. I brought you flowers and magazines and made sure you never got lonely and never thought twice about any of it because my best friend could have died and I couldn't imagine doing anything else or being anywhere else."

I sank back into the couch, the force of her words piling on top of me, pushing me down into the cushions. Amanda and I hadn't fought since third grade, when I accidentally left her back door open and her cat Curry wandered outside. Her family couldn't find him for two days, and she spent those forty-eight hours alternating between calling me horrible names and ignoring me. But when Curry showed up with a dead lizard in his mouth on their front porch by the weekend, it was like it had never happened, and we'd never fought again.

So now it was like nine years of frustration, disappointment, and sadness were pouring out from behind whatever dam she'd been keeping them behind, and I was drowning in the tidal wave.

"You know what friends *don't* do?" She wasn't yelling, but this harsh quiet was worse. It cut even deeper. "Friends don't ditch friends when they get hot boyfriends and start going to parties and hanging out with the water polo team and being *popular.* Friends don't suddenly think they're too good for the person who has been there with them through everything. So don't talk to me about being insensitive, okay?"

I couldn't believe she was bringing this up now. Couldn't she see how upset I was? Ditching her for some party was nothing compared to being paralyzed. Why would she try to make me feel worse than I already did? "Amanda—"

"No. You stop. I get that you're upset about your legs. God, I really do. And I'm trying here. Give me a break, okay? At least I'm trying. Where are your other friends now?"

Tears welled up in my eyes. I opened my mouth to say something, anything, that would hurt her like she'd hurt me by pointing out how everyone left me. How Curt had left me.

Jack put his hand gently on my arm. "Kara, I think that you're—"

"Of course you're on her side, Jack. That's fine." I couldn't handle whatever he had to say. I'd disappointed him again, I knew it. For the second time this week, in fact, and I couldn't even deal with it. I don't know why it was hurting so much;

it was just Jack. But the look on his face made me feel hollow inside. Like I'd lost something. "I'm getting used to being all alone over here."

He squeezed my arm, but I whipped it out of his grip before I had a chance to register the warmth of his hand and left him staring down at his empty fingers. "I'm not on anyone's side," he said. "I totally understand where you're coming from, I just think—"

"I don't care what you think. I really don't."

It was a lie, but I didn't know what else to say.

Mom had apparently been eavesdropping from the kitchen and had enough of our drama. She came back into the room, her arms crossed. "Okay, Jack. Amanda. Kara's had a long day. I think maybe it's time you two leave and let her get some rest for now, okay?"

"God, Mom," I snapped. "They don't have to go. I was just—"

But Amanda and Jack were already standing up, cleaning up the plates and napkins, and walking into the kitchen. "No," Amanda said, "your mom's right. We should go."

Irritation mixed with regret, and it flooded my insides. "Don't leave, you guys. I didn't mean it."

But they didn't listen to me. Mom helped them pick up the dinner trash and walked them to the door. "Thanks for the pizza," she said as she ushered them out the door. "We'll see you two soon. Drive safe." The door clicked shut, and it was only a matter of seconds before Mom was back in the TV room.

"What was that all about?" She didn't sound angry; she sounded defeated. Like she didn't even know what to do with me anymore. "Is that any way to treat your friends?"

Resting my elbows on my thighs, I covered my face with my hands, as if I could hide from this flood of shame that was crashing down on me all of a sudden. "I don't know," I said. "They're the only people who have stayed my friends this whole time and I'm being terrible to them. What's wrong with me?"

"I don't know, sweetie," Mom said. She came over and hugged me, for the first time since I'd been home, stroking my hair soothingly. I leaned in to her, and she hugged me harder. "I don't know."

"This isn't me," I said. "I hate it." I hadn't truly felt like myself since the accident, and on top of that, the cocktail o' meds wasn't really making things any better. Pills for this, pills for that, and they were all impacting my personality. The painkillers weren't so bad, but it was the antidepressants that made me feel off. Foggy. I'd tried two different types now, but neither one was right. No matter what I tried, they were throwing off the balance of what made me who I was.

Mom let out a long sigh and sat down on the couch, facing me. "I just wish you weren't so sad and mad all the time, sweetie. I know things are terrible, but there are people who are way worse off than you. You could be quadriplegic. You could have lost a limb. You could have died in that accident."

My instinct was to snap at her that just because things could have been worse, it didn't mean that they weren't bad. And I knew it could have been worse. I'd spent almost every single night reading the stories of people who posted on the disabilities message boards I'd found online. Some people were born without being able to move any of their limbs, ever. Some people had been in accidents ten times more horrific than mine, and had external injuries as well. Some

people had lost every single person they ever cared about in
the accidents that left them alive but forever changed. Of
course things could be worse, and I was learning that first-
hand. But that didn't mean that things weren't tough for me.

Instead of saying what I wanted to, though, I took a deep
breath and let it out slowly. Then I took another one, and I
nodded. "Maybe we can try switching up my medication
again?"

"Sure." Mom patted my arm. "I'll call the doctor."

That night I had a hard time falling asleep, and my normal routine of message board reading wasn't helping. No
one online had the answers I was looking for.

Sitting around and wishing for my legs to magically
work again was pointless. That just wasn't going to happen,
and I was going to make myself miserable if that was all I
cared about. All I focused on.

Just because I couldn't walk, didn't mean I couldn't have
a life. It didn't mean I had nothing to be happy about.

But how could I be fulfilled in my life without dancing?
It was tied in to the core of who I was, and who I'd been for
as long as I could remember knowing myself. Is this how
people felt when they lost a loved one? My grandma died
when I was younger, but she was sick for a long time before
that. I had time to get used to her passing. This was different.
This was the sudden and absolute murder of the one thing
that made me who I was. Kara Moore was a dancer. Everyone
knew that. Sure, I was also a student and a daughter and a
friend and a girlfriend. I was pretty smart and usually nice
and I had shiny hair and I'd help people with their homework. But above all those things, I was a dancer.

Until I wasn't anymore.

It was impossible to imagine myself any other way, as much as I was trying to change things. Dancing was in every square inch of the future I'd imagined for myself. I didn't know how to be Kara without being a dancer.

This wasn't just mourning the loss of my legs; it was mourning the death of the person I thought I'd become. And that was the hardest part. Even more difficult than being in the chair.

Mom and I thought that the third time would be the charm with the antidepressants, that the new round of meds would make me feel better, and in some ways they did. I felt less cloudy, less numb to everything, which was definitely an improvement. But while I was feeling better in some ways, I was feeling worse in others.

I hadn't heard from Jack and Amanda since I'd yelled at them. I knew I owed them an apology, but I couldn't bring myself to say the words. It was too hard to put myself out there like that, and I had so many difficult things going on in my life, I didn't know if I had it in me to deal with one more.

But without the two of them around to keep my negativity in check and act as a buffer between me and people who didn't think before they opened their big mouths, I was getting worse and worse at humoring people, especially strangers and their unsolicited comments about my chair. The worst was a run-in with Maria Luna, the girl who sat in front of me in Government. She turned to me after the bell rang as we both collected our books, getting ready to head to lunch, and said, "I swear, Kara. You're such an inspiration!" It wasn't a new comment. I'd heard it so many times from so many people that it didn't even matter who said it; it was always the same. They called me an inspiration or strong or brave and I smiled and nodded even though I didn't understand why they said it or what made me inspirational or strong or brave, especially when I was just, like, going to lunch or something, and they left feeling better about themselves for making Wheelchair Girl feel good about her Sad Life.

I was literally the same person I was before the accident; I just used a wheelchair to get around now. But I was a little moodier than Old Kara, a little more depressed, and on a lot more pills, which made me react a little bit differently to the question this time.

"Why?"

Maria was clearly taken aback by the question. "You know," she said, smiling and waving at my chair.

"So—" I folded my hands over the pile of books in my lap. "—I'm an inspiration because some stupid drunk A-hole got in his car and happened to hit me?"

"Oh, no." She shook her head and waved her hands back and forth. "That's not what I meant. I meant, you know, because you come to school every day in your wheelchair..."

I cocked my head to the side and narrowed my eyes at her. "So, I'm an inspiration because I'm *not* a high school dropout? I should've quit school because I have a spinal cord injury?"

"Well, no, I'm just saying..." She started backing away from me.

I scooted my chair forward. "So, why am I an inspiration because I got in an accident? Jeff Ahmed was in that boat accident last year. Was he an inspiration? Because he got a concussion and then came back to school?"

She wrung her hands and her forehead wrinkled. "Well, no. But his accident—"

"At what point does continuing to appear in public after an accident make you an inspiration? Would I be an inspiration if I had a cast? Or does it have to be a permanent injury?" Oh my God, what was wrong with me? I'd never said more than two words to Maria Luna in my life, and here I was going off on her when she was trying to be nice. But just because she was trying to be nice didn't mean she *was* nice. And why did I have to sit here and smile at everyone who told me how strong I was?

She threw her backpack over her shoulder and rolled her eyes. "God, Kara. Forget I said anything. I had no idea this whole thing made you so bitter."

"Bitter?" I laughed. "You think this is me being bitter? Girl, you have no idea what bitter looks like." *Stop it, Kara. You're making it worse. Stop talking.* But I couldn't. I was on autopilot.

Maria opened her mouth to reply, but apparently I wasn't done yet. Words flew out of my mouth before I even had a chance to think them up, like the past weeks of confusion and pain and frustration were all being dumped on poor Maria Luna.

"This is me being irritated that everyone treats me like some poster child for Strength and Courage because something crappy happened to me and I didn't curl up in a ball and quit life. What would you do if this happened to you? Stay in your room forever? Kill yourself? Of course not. You'd get up and go to school, even though everyone looks at you and talks about you and treats you like they haven't known you since you were five. You'd do the same thing. I'm not an inspiration and I'm not bitter, I'm just Kara and I'm normal and trying to get through the day, just like anyone else."

"God. Whatever," she said, and walked out the door. But I wasn't done with the conversation. Venting about these random comments I'd been getting since coming back to school felt so amazing. I swear, I was ten pounds lighter from getting that off my chest. I wanted to keep going, but the classroom was empty now.

I let out a sigh. *Of course it is,* I thought. *I was driving everyone away.*

The accident changed my body, and I had no control over that. But it looked like it was also changing who I was. I kept saying I was still me, but it looked like I was morphing from a girl who was friendly and likable to this person who went off on random classmates until they ran away.

And went off on the only people who were there for me. My only friends.

That was something I could do something about. I needed to. Because I couldn't live the rest of my life like this.

That afternoon, I was so lonely after school that I was about to maybe break down and actually read *Pride and Prejudice.* But instead I was dwelling on my run-in with Maria and wishing I had someone to sort it out with. Without thinking about it, I grabbed my phone from my side table and texted Amanda.

I MISS PATRICK

I probably should have said something real instead of bringing our stuffed bear into it, but we both had such a soft spot for that silly toy. Mentioning him would get Amanda right in the feels.

Which it obviously had, because my phone vibrated with a text back not even a minute later. PATRICK LOVES YOU, KARA, it said. After another second, another text flashed across the screen. AND SO DO I.

I stared at my phone as the words sank in. She loved me no matter what. No matter how awfully I had treated her before and no matter what had been taken from me and no matter what my future held, Amanda loved me for who I was. And she might say or do thoughtless things every now and then, but she was trying. And that was more than I could say for a lot of people.

In fact, it was more than I could say for myself.

I'M SORRY I SNAPPED AT YOU.

I had so much else I wanted to say to her. How I didn't know how to be myself anymore, and how I don't even know why I got so mad. How I don't know how I could have done any of this without her support, and how terrible and endless the past few days had been without her. Instead I just added THANKS FOR EVERYTHING and hit Send. I knew she'd understand.

And while I had my phone in my hand, I decided to text Jack, too.

HOPEFULLY I'LL BE MYSELF AGAIN SOON. I MISS YOU.

It took only a second for him to reply.

I'LL BE HERE NO MATTER WHAT.

CHAPTER 16

It was amazing that Jack and Amanda still wanted to hang out with me after how awful I'd been to them. But now that our cooling-off period was over, Amanda found me during passing period the next day at school and said, "Tonight. I'm bringing over the DVD of *Pitch Perfect*, Jack's bringing ice cream, and we're going to work on homework and chill. Sound like a plan?"

I wanted to apologize to her face for what I'd said to her or thank her for knowing exactly what I needed, but she cut me off as soon as I opened my mouth. "I have to spend lunch in media tech, but you can iron out details with Jack, okay? See you tonight!" The tardy bell rang, cutting off any further conversation, and she rushed off, her braids flapping behind her.

Later that night, I searched through the kitchen for a snack to hold me over until Amanda and Jack came by, Logan curled up on my lap, when Dad walked into the kitchen from the garage.

"You're home early," I said. "It's not even dark yet."

"I know. Crazy, huh?" He tossed his keys on the kitchen table, and the sound made Logan lift his head and let out a small, rumbly bark. "I figured I could get the rest of my work done tomorrow, so I came home to see you." He leaned over and gave Logan a pat, then kissed me on the cheek. He was about to straighten up when he leaned over again and wrapped his arms around my shoulders in a tight hug. "So, tell me about your day," he said, sitting down at the kitchen table.

Dad and I talked for over an hour. I filled him in on all my classes, how life at school was going, and how I'd treated Amanda and Jack. I couldn't think of the last time the two of us had talked like this, not even before the accident. I hated that it took me getting hurt to get him to make the effort to come home early and hang out with me, but if this was a positive side effect of my accident, I would take it.

Finally, I bit the side of my lip and mumbled, "I think I should start going to therapy."

Dad's eyebrows shot up to his hairline. "Why do you say that?"

I explained what happened with my friends and with Maria, and how I was feeling less and less like myself, like the person I was before the accident. "I don't know." I let out a long sigh. "I just can't let it take everything from me, you know? I think talking to someone might help."

Dad hugged me again. "I think that's an excellent idea. We'll call your doctor and get some recommendations first thing in the morning."

And just like that, some of the hardness my heart had

been carrying around softened. It was only a little bit, a small crack in the shell, but it was something.

After talking to me for a while longer, Dad went upstairs to shower, and as I cleaned up the kitchen, the front door creaked open and Jack called, "Hello!" Logan jumped off my lap, barking, and ran to the front door to fulfill his job as official greeting committee.

"Hey, guys," I called back. "I'm in here. Come in!"

But it wasn't both of them who showed up in the kitchen a minute later, it was only Jack, a plastic grocery store bag in his hand, Logan at his heels. "So, good news, bad news, worse news. What do you want first?"

"Uh, good news?"

He lifted the bag in the air. "I have bacon ice cream! Hooray!"

I laughed. "So, the bad news and worse news?"

"Bad news? Amanda got called in to work at the theater tonight."

I'd been bracing myself for actual bad news, so when he told me that it would only be the two of us again, no Amanda, my shoulders relaxed and I leaned back in my chair. What was he talking about? I wouldn't call that *bad* news.

"Why are you smiling? I haven't even told you the worse news. She had the DVD, and I didn't have time to grab a replacement." He smiled. "But did I mention I have bacon ice cream?"

"Bacon ice cream trumps all," I said. "Make yourself useful and scoop us some. I'll figure out the movie situation."

I left Jack in the kitchen and wheeled myself to the TV room, thinking about my own DVD collection, which was mostly dance movies, plus Pixar movies I'd seen a million times, my dad's bloody action films, and my mom's romantic comedies. None of these were anything I wanted to watch with Jack.

"I have nothing to watch," I said when he came back into the room holding our two bowls. "Unless you want to watch *Up* for the millionth time."

"Ugh," he said. "I love that movie, but I swear, that's what every single teacher shows on movie days. I feel like I can recite it from memory."

I shrugged. "Well, I guess we can see what's on TV."

"Let's go outside," he said. "Let's just eat our ice cream on the deck. Americans spend an average of, like, thirty-four hours watching TV, you know. We should get some air and stuff instead. It's such a nice night."

It *was* a nice night. There was a chill in the air, as there had been for the past few weeks. But it was still warm enough to be outside, even with the cool breeze. Jack grabbed blankets and covered me with one when I found the ideal spot to situate myself right next to the big deck chair, and he closed the sliding glass door before Logan could dart out into the yard.

"It's a little chilly," he said, handing me my bowl and getting comfy on the chair. "But, whatever. We should enjoy it while we can."

"Exactly," I said. "I think it's awesome."

We sat in silence for a minute or two, eating our ice cream, before he said, "Is everything okay, Kara? I mean, are you okay? I've been worried about you this past week."

I let out a long sigh. "I guess. I don't know. I'm just trying to figure all of this out." I waved my hand over my legs.

"It's okay if you don't have everything figured out, you

know. It hasn't been that long since the accident. I know how much you like to have things in order, but I think it's okay to take a little time to get stuff figured out. No one expects you to be perfect at all of this already."

"Everyone keeps telling me things happen for a reason. There has to be a reason this happened to me, Jack. I can't just lose everything and have it mean nothing."

He reached his hand toward me, but he quickly pulled it back and dropped it on his lap. "You didn't lose everything. You have Amanda." He coughed. "And me."

I looked at him, trying to figure out what was going on with him. Jack felt different today. And as someone who was a bit of a Jack Matthews expert, I couldn't place this look on his face.

"Oh my God," he said, snapping me out of my study of his expression. "I think it's starting to rain."

I turned back to the yard to see he was right. Soft rain had started to fall, and I stuck my hand out, water softly beating against my palm.

But when I turned to Jack, expecting to see him staring out at the drops falling gently from the sky, he was actually looking at me.

"What?"

He cleared his throat in that very deliberate way and shifted on the bench. "Can I tell you something? You promise you won't get mad?"

"Um, no. I have no idea what you're going to say, but when you lead with that, there's about a ninety-eight percent chance that it's going to make me mad no matter what I promise."

He looked so uncomfortable that I thought for sure he

was going to avoid looking at me. But instead of focusing his eyes on my foot or my arm or the rain spattering on the deck, he looked right into my eyes.

"It was me who made sure your name stayed on the ballot for Homecoming."

"What? What do you mean?"

"When you were in the hospital, we were going through the list of nominees. Mrs. Mendoza was checking everyone's grades and detentions and everything to make sure they were all qualified to be in the running. And when we got to you, everyone thought it was weird to leave you on. They all said we should ask water polo to pick another nominee. But I told them they had to leave your name on there and not let water polo pick someone else even if they wanted to."

"I don't get it. Why would you do that?"

He scooted his chair closer to me, and he reached over and grabbed my hand, squeezing my fingers. "Because you deserved it, Kara."

Irritation crept into my voice. "I'm not—"

"I know what you're going to say, but you don't deserve it because you're in a wheelchair. You know I don't think about it that way. But you went through a bunch of crap, and after being in the hospital for so long, you deserved to be in a pretty dress and a crown with everyone cheering for you. But, honestly, you deserved that even before you got in your accident. You always have."

I shook my head. "That's sweet, Jack. It really is. But look at me. I'm not exactly Homecoming Queen material these days."

"Stop it," he said, his voice suddenly serious. "You look beautiful. You always do."

"Oh, please," I said. "Aside from the fact that I am stuck

in this chair, my hair is all over the place, I have no makeup on, I look like I just rolled out of bed. Literally." I laughed, and I looked at him, expecting him to laugh along with me. But there was no laughter on his end, just a look of serious concentration.

And before I even knew what was happening, Jack leaned in toward me, covering the short distance between us quickly, and he kissed me.

I'd forgotten how soft Jack's lips were. How he would smile into my mouth while he kissed me, like this was the most fun he could possibly be having.

I'd forgotten how kissing him was the best kind of familiar. Like coming home.

So, before I realized what was happening, I kissed him back. My hand tangled up in the curly ends of his hair, and my fingers pushed his beanie back on his head. His hand pressed down on my shoulder, and he used it to pull himself closer to me. We kissed and kissed, and I lost myself in the pressure of his lips on mine and the feeling of his hands on my face, my shoulders, my back. His hand trailed down my arm, leaving a trail of goose bumps in its wake.

And then I couldn't feel his hand anymore.

I pulled back from him, breaking our kiss, and saw his hand resting on my leg.

Something about the sensation of his lips still lingering on mine and the rain, falling harder now, and the sight of his hand resting on my leg, but me not being able to feel it at all—well, it all sent hot whips of panic through my body. All of a sudden I didn't know which way was up.

"You need to go," I said. Panic flooded me, and I was shaking.

"What?" he said, his voice full of confusion. "Why?"

I shook my head, but it only made the conflicting thoughts pinball around even faster. "We shouldn't have done this."

Jack drew his eyebrows together in concern. "Kara, what's wrong? Are you okay?"

I looked at my shaky hands. "What's wrong is that you're only doing this because you feel sorry for me."

"No, I—"

"And it's not me you're kissing, it's the old me." I turned my hands over in my lap, but I kept staring at them, trying to will them to be still. I couldn't look up. I couldn't look at him. "But that Kara doesn't exist anymore, okay? She's gone. So if you have it in your head that I'm that girl anymore, if you're doing this because you never moved on when we broke up before, then you need to go. Right now."

"What are you even talking about?"

"My leg," I said. Tears sprang to my eyes, and I swallowed hard to keep them from falling. "You had your hand on my leg. Like I could feel you touching me or something."

"I'm sorry if that bothered you," he said. He rose from the bench and moved right in front of me, squatting down so our heads were on the same level. "But, Kara, I love your legs. I love your legs because they're part of you."

"Don't say that." I shook my head. "You don't have to say that."

"I'm saying it because it's the truth. I never stopped being in love with you, Kara. I was in love with you the day you broke up with me, and I was in love with you the day of your accident, and I was in love with you the day you woke up in the hospital. Nothing has changed that. Not your legs, not your chair, nothing."

I didn't realize until that moment how much I'd been aching to hear these words from someone. My mom, Curt, anyone. But I also didn't realize that I already knew that Jack felt this way, and that he didn't even need to say it, because he'd been showing me since the second I woke up in the hospital. Jack supported me and lifted me up and never once treated me like I was anything but myself. He'd been here all along, loving me and seeing me as Kara and not Wheelchair Girl this whole time, and I'd been so caught up in my own drama, I hadn't even noticed.

And I hadn't noticed how much I felt the exact same way.

But now I noticed. And now I leaned forward and kissed him, with the rain falling on us from all sides. And he leaned forward, hands on my knees, and kissed me back.

CHAPTER 17

"Are you ready to do this?"

On Friday morning, Jack, Amanda, and I headed into
school with a plan. Jack ended up staying at my house the
night before until my dad finally kicked him out at close to
midnight. And we were only kissing for about half the time.
Maybe 65 percent. The rest of the time was spent plotting,
Internet searching, and filling in Amanda on the plan via
text while she sold popcorn and Sour Patch Kids at the theater.

"I'm ready." I sat up as straight as possible in my chair.
"Let's do this."

The three of us maneuvered through the morning campus crowds, much more confident than the first time we did
this two weeks prior. So much had changed in those two
weeks, and I had changed, too. I could tell by the way I held
myself in my chair, posture straight, shoulders back, and the

way I was looking around me as I wheeled through the
school, not down at the ground. Not trying to disappear.

Trying to be seen.

"Here we are," Jack said, pulling open the door of the activities office.

"I'm ready." Amanda steadied her video camera and
clicked it on. "Recording."

"Okay, here we go." And I wheeled myself into the office,
where Mrs. Mendoza was talking to another student behind
the desk.

"Good morning, Kara. Jack." She wrinkled her nose in
confusion when she saw Amanda and her camera, but we
didn't give her a chance to ask any questions.

"Mrs. Mendoza," I said, not letting my voice waver even
though it wanted to. "I want you to put me back on the Homecoming ballot."

Her face fell, and lines of concern creased into her forehead. "Oh, hon, I'm sorry. I can't do that. When you gave up
your nomination, water polo nominated someone else in your
place." She picked up her clipboard and ran her finger down
the paper on the front of it. "It looks like . . . yes, they nominated Jenny Roy."

It was what I'd expected to hear, but I couldn't help but
flinch when I heard her name. I guess some part of me had
been hoping that they didn't replace me, or didn't replace me
with her, but that part of me was pretty ridiculous.

"That's okay, Mrs. Mendoza," Jack said. He reached into
his back pocket and pulled out a sheet of paper that had been
folded into a small square. He spread it out in the desk in front
of her, using both hands to attempt to smooth it out. "I'm
starting a new club. Here's all the paperwork right here. And

my first order of business is to nominate Kara Moore as my club's Homecoming Queen nominee."

Now the lines of concern on Mrs. Mendoza's face smoothed out, and her eyebrows drew together. "Now, Jack. You're the Commissioner of Clubs for Student Government. You know the rules. You can't start up a club just to nominate someone for Homecoming. It doesn't work that way."

I noticed him steal a look at Amanda, who gave a tiny nod without moving the camera. Yeah, she was getting this.

"Of course I know that. But this isn't a club we're starting just to nominate Kara. It's a school chapter of the Walk and Roll Foundation."

"We want to raise awareness of the realities of spinal cord injuries and the dangers of drunk driving with the students here on campus," I said. "And the Homecoming fund-raiser is the perfect place to start."

When I dropped out of the running for Homecoming before, a big part of it was because I didn't want to represent water polo and fund-raise for a bunch of guys who wanted nothing to do with me now that I was in a wheelchair. Curt grabbed his first opportunity to distance himself from me, and I wanted to get as far away from him as I could, too. But Jack had the idea of starting a chapter of a club that really mattered to me and representing that. Doing Homecoming on my own terms. After a lot of research online, we found Walk and Roll, a foundation that's all about raising awareness for spinal cord injuries and educating teens on the dangers of drunk and distracted driving. As soon as I started reading about Walk and Roll, I completely changed my mind about this whole Homecoming thing. Fund-raising to get a club on campus to raise drunk-driving awareness—now, that was the way to get me more enthusiastic about putting my-self out there as a queen nominee.

Mrs. Mendoza scanned Jack's paperwork. "I don't know, you guys," she said, shaking her head. "You know how the Homecoming fund-raisers are. They're silly and lighthearted. Remember last year? Tegan Foster and the drama depart-ment did a fund-raiser to repaint the mascot's loincloth on the mural outside the theater. Don't get me wrong—I think this is a completely worthy cause, and a fantastic club to have on campus. And I can see why it's so important to you, Kara. It's just . . . I don't think Homecoming is the time or place for this type of fund-raiser. Isn't it something you want people to take seriously?"

"That's why we think people will really pay attention," I said. "We think that by being the one serious fund-raiser of the bunch, we can really get people thinking about drunk driving. I know I'm not going to win. But I think I have an opportunity here to make an impact and really open the eyes of some people here on campus, you know?"

A line of wrinkles formed on Mrs. Mendoza's forehead as she glanced over Jack's paperwork one more time. Then she looked to her left, where Amanda stood, quietly filming every-thing, and finally her eyes traveled down to me. Me and my chair.

"Fine," she said. "But don't say that I didn't warn you when this becomes weird." She picked up the clipboard again and scribbled on the bottom of her master list. "Now, there's a meeting after school today in the gym for all the nominees, so make sure you're there, okay, Kara?"

"Oh, we'll be there," I said. And by "we," I meant the ador-able boy who was hugging me like his life depended on it, and the awesome girl behind the camera who was beaming and giving me a thumbs-up.

Amanda met me outside the room for the Homecoming meeting after school, camera in hand.

"You know that me following you around with this thing—" She waved the camera in my face. "— is only going to bring more attention to you, right?"

Jack, who turned out to be full of great plans last night, gave Amanda the idea of switching topics for the media class scholarship project, and she had been completely on board. She acted like she'd do pretty much anything to avoid the cross-country team, but I knew she was super pumped about showing how active a disabled high school student could be. She'd follow me around during my Homecoming campaign, going to physical therapy, adjusting to life in my wheelchair, and film the whole thing for her project, which she would edit into an awesome documentary-style video that met all the requirements of the scholarship contest. It would help her to have a totally original project that she was so much more invested in than the cross-country team, and it would help me pump up awareness for our new chapter of Walk and Roll and raise funds for drunk-driving education in the school and the community. It was pretty fantastic for everyone.

So, I was okay with the extra eyeballs on me, since it was all for a good cause.

Well, most of the eyeballs. The only unwelcome ones were Jenny Roy's.

Any truce that might have passed between me and Jenny Roy on my first day back was broken the second I entered the room for the Homecoming meeting after school, which was slowly filling up with the other nominees. Instead of ignoring me, as she had every time I saw her around campus over the past week or so, she shot daggers at me with her eyes. When I smiled at her in an attempt to be friendly, she jumped up from her chair, literally pushed a girl out of her way, and crossed the distance between the two of us within seconds.

She opened her mouth to say something, but before she could, I noticed her shoot a glance at Amanda and her camera, and Amanda lifted her hand and waved at Jenny. I laughed at this, especially because Jenny's face started to twitch as the wheels turned in her simple little head. Would she let the camera keep her from saying the awful things she wanted to say to me? Knowing our past, how she never let anything stop her before, probably not. Apparently, her solution was to step closer to me, so she was practically in my lap, and lower her voice—as if that could keep Amanda's camera from picking up her vitriol.

"What are you doing here?" she spat at me. "Didn't you get the memo? I'm water polo's nominee now."

"Didn't *you* get the memo? I didn't want to represent water polo anymore. I gave up the nomination. So, you know, you're welcome." Okay, so I let a little bit of snark creep out through my voice. I couldn't help it.

Her eyebrows drew together, wrinkling her forehead. "Just because you're confined to a wheelchair, you think—"

I gave her the sympathetic head tilt. "No, you have it backwards. The wheelchair is what keeps me from being confined somewhere. If I didn't have it, I'd be confined to my house." I patted the wheels of my chair and smiled. "I'm super grateful for my chair, actually. It's not something I'm stuck in like some kind of prison."

"Whatever," she said. "I know you think you can turn Homecoming into your own personal soapbox, but here's a newsflash for you: No one cares, okay? You're not the big deal you think you are, Kara, and no one wants a depressing Homecoming full of PSAs and life lessons and charity work and whatever other nonsense fund-raiser you have going on. Stop trying to make everyone feel bad for you all the time and let us have fun."

Anger bubbled up under my skin, ready to burst. Like I wanted people to feel bad for me. Like I wanted everything to be about my chair. None of this had been my choice.

Everything inside me wanted to explode at Jenny.

But I thought back to my argument with Curt when I first came back to school. I had been upset, and I really let him get to me. I went crazy and made a scene, and even though Curt had been a total dick to me in front of everyone, I was the one who left embarrassed.

I didn't give two effs about Jenny Roy or what she said or thought about me. She obviously wanted some kind of fight, but I wasn't going to let her get to me like that. I wouldn't give her the satisfaction.

So, instead of picking one of the colorful insults flying through my head to throw back at her like a grenade, I folded my hands on my lap and smiled. "Good luck with your fund-raiser, Jenny. I hope it's wildly successful."

Then, as the meeting was about to begin, I pushed myself away from her, over to the other end of the room, so I could find out exactly what I'd need to do to win Homecoming and roll over Jenny Roy on my way there.

CHAPTER 18

"If I'm wincing in pain, you need to turn off the camera, okay? No ugly face on video." I settled into my chair in the parking lot as Amanda slammed her trunk closed and locked up her car. The hospital had referred me to a new physical therapy center that focused specifically on spinal cord injuries, and Amanda was tagging along on this visit to get some footage for her video.

Amanda accompanying me to physical therapy was like worlds colliding, but she said it would make her project better to show me being active in multiple ways. Better video project, better Homecoming campaign, better chance of beating Jenny Roy, better chance of making more money for our project.

"Deal," she said. "Now, let's do this. You hold the camera pointed at yourself and I'll push you up to PT while I interview you, okay?"

I told her how to get to the physical therapy room at the medical center, and I positioned the camera so it was facing me, selfie-style.

"So, Kara," Amanda said in her best investigative-journalist voice. "What do you want to get out of physical therapy? Do you have a specific goal, or is it for general recovery and well-being?"

"I want to walk again." I didn't think about my answer for a second; it just leapt from my mouth like it had a life of its own.

It's not like I'd been spending time thinking specifically about walking. Between my parents, Jack, Homecoming, and all the drama at school, I'd had enough on my mind as it was. Especially because it wasn't something I'd thought was possible. Dr. Nguyen told me I would never walk again.

The end.

But deep in my heart, in the place I kept my wildest hopes and craziest secrets, it was what I wanted. I wanted to be able to walk.

And, even more, I wanted to dance.

"Do you think that will happen?" Amanda asked.

I let out a long sigh. "Well, nothing will happen if I just sit in my chair, right? If I accept the fact that my legs are never going to work again, then they aren't, for sure. But if I work hard at PT and do everything in my power, then maybe there's a chance. It might take twenty years or forty years, but I need to start now, and work for it every day."

Amanda pushed me through the automatic doors, and we followed the hallway down to the PT room.

"I want my life to be full of possibilities, not regret, you know?"

"That's a sound bite if I've ever heard one." Amanda leaned over my shoulder so her face was in the lens of the camera, smooshed up right next to mine. "Note to self: Self, put that in, for sure."

I made a face at the camera, and I handed it back to her. Pushing my shoulders back, I wheeled myself into the PT room, Amanda followed with her camera, and the first person I saw was Ana, saying good bye to the techs and gathering her things.

"Kara!" She wore her usual smile, like physical therapy on her paralyzed legs was the most fun she could imagine having today.

"You're coming here now?" I asked. "How was your PT session?"

She rolled her eyes. "Yeah. Sometimes I think they're trying to kill me. But in a good way, I guess."

I introduced Amanda to Ana and explained the video project. Ana, who was still in middle school, hung on every word, like high school Homecoming was everything the movies and TV shows told her it would be. I guess my story did have a lot of drama.

"Kara's going to be Homecoming Queen," Amanda said, smiling.

Ana clapped excitedly. "Oh my God, really? I want to see pictures! Will you show me pictures?"

Amanda chimed in with a singsong voice, "And Kara has a boooy-friend, so—"

"You have a boyfriend?" Ana squealed. "Tell me! Do you have a picture?"

Heat rushed to my cheeks. Jack made sure to tell me before he left my house after we'd kissed that he wanted to be my boyfriend again, and I had agreed. And, of course, the second he was out the door, I'd called Amanda and filled her in on the details. She'd been relieved to hear that Jack finally made his move; apparently, he'd been asking her for advice on how to go for it since my first day back at school. She'd even faked that stupid popcorn sickness after our mall date to give us some alone time so he'd do something about it. I'd been worried that our new couple status might upset the Kara–Amanda–Jack balance, but we'd done this threesome before with no issues, and it was like falling back into a familiar pattern. It was comforting to know that some things could go back to how they used to be.

I was about to try to explain our situation to Ana, but a tall man with a mustache poked his head in the room before I could even begin. "Ana," he said. "Time to go, *mija*."

Ana smiled. "That's my dad. I have to go. But you'll tell me about your boyfriend the next time we run into each other, okay, Kara?"

"Or just give me your number," I said. "I'll text you." Somewhere in the middle of all this, even though she was so much younger than me, Ana had become an actual friend. Going through all these wheelchair adventures together could really bond you to someone, I guess, and it was pretty awesome to have someone who could really understand it, even if she was still in middle school. She was like the real-life version of all the people on the disability message boards I'd come to count on every night before I went to sleep. She understood the sometimes-conflicting, always-confusing feelings I had about life in a wheelchair, and she got me in ways Jack and Amanda and my parents never would, no matter how hard they tried.

As Ana rolled herself out the door, she turned her head back to face me. "Last time I saw you, you looked really sad."

I nodded. "I was."

"Before my accident, my dad and I fought all the time. He was never around. But it's crazy. Now that he has to help me out so much, and I guess he thought he might not make it or something, things have totally changed between us." She shrugged. "I'm not glad I got hurt, but I'm glad to have my dad back, you know?"

I knew what she meant. There was no way I would have realized my feelings for Jack if it hadn't been for my accident. I'd still be with Curt, who sucked. It took this drastic, world altering event for me to realize the awesome thing that was right in front of me all along.

Even though Amanda had driven me to PT, my parents asked if they could pick me up and take me out to dinner. Things had been odd in my house over the past few days, and their insistence on family time was leaving me a little uneasy.

The fight my parents had the night of my accident, and my mom's confession about their possible divorce, was never far from my mind. And for good reason, because as soon as I settled myself in the car, I could sense weirdness, so obvious that it was almost like a fourth passenger, buckled up next to me.

"Is everything okay?" I asked.

But instead of answering, Mom asked, "How was PT today?"

Mom hadn't asked about it before, since it seemed like her mission in life was to avoid, avoid, avoid, so I jumped at the opportunity to tell her how it was going. "Amanda got most of it on video, actually, so you can watch it. I'm not making a ton of progress yet——"

"But it's still early," Dad broke in. "It's only been a month. Tiny progress you make now snowballs as you go, and you'll be wheeling circles around that place in no time."

Or walking, I thought, and I smiled at the possibility.

The weirdness from the car followed us into the restaurant, my favorite Mexican place with the best chips and salsa ever. There was no conversation as we perused the menus and ordered our dinner, and I watched through narrowed eyes as Mom and Dad shifted around and coughed and looked anywhere but at me.

"Okay, please just tell me what's up," I said when I couldn't take the heavy silence for another second. "I can tell something is going on with you guys. Whatever it is, I can handle it." I didn't know if I *could* handle the reality of my parents getting a divorce, but I could handle it more easily than them keeping it from me and acting all shifty. The longer they hid things, the more my overactive imagination took over, and right now I was picturing the messiest divorce and custody battle this side of a daytime soap. There was no way the truth could be that bad. At least I hoped not, anyway.

Dad cleared his throat and Mom shifted around in her seat some more.

"Well," Dad said, poking at the ice in his water with his straw. "You know your mother and I have been having some . . . difficulties."

Here it was. I nodded, gripping the wheels of my chair until my hands started to tingle.

"I don't know if you remember the conversation we had right before your accident," Mom said, reaching across the table with her hand outstretched.

I nodded again, afraid to speak, and placed my hand in hers.

She smiled. "Sweetie, you have inspired us."

I yanked my hand away and rolled my eyes. I was in no mood to deal with this crap from my parents, too. "God, Mom. Don't—"

"Just listen to me," she said. "I know you were struggling. With your chair, with your medication, and with all the feelings that came along with all of this. But you didn't accept that. You wanted to do everything you could to feel normal again, even if it meant admitting you needed help and going to therapy."

"That inspired me and your mother, Kara," Dad said. "It really did." Now he reached across the table and grabbed Mom's hand, smiling at her. "So while you were at PT today, we went to our first session of marriage counseling."

"What?" I blinked at him, trying to make sense of what he was telling me. "So you're *not* getting a divorce?" I didn't realize I'd been carrying the thought of my parents splitting up around with me like a weight on my lap, but the second my dad said counseling, I felt instantly lighter. Unburdened.

"We don't know what the future holds right now. But I promise you that we're going to try to work on our problems before we let it come to that," Mom said.

"We know it's not going to be easy." Dad reached his free hand across the table and grabbed my hand, so we looked like we were about to start a prayer circle or something. "Things aren't going to magically get better for us, sweetie. But we're going to work hard on it. And we'll need your help to work on our relationship as a family. Can you help us out?"

I smiled. It was a smile so big that it actually hurt.

No divorce.

And the crazy thing was, if I hadn't gotten in an accident that night, this might never have happened. My parents would have divorced for sure. My family would have imploded, and there would have been nothing to prompt them to try to work things out.

Maybe good things could grow from the ashes of destruction. Maybe this accident was the end of my old life, but it was also the beginning of a new one. And maybe that new one had the potential to be okay after all.

CHAPTER 19

"Amanda, stop drooling over the competition," Jack said, smacking her on the arm. "You're not helping our cause that way." The last few days before Homecoming were the fund-raising days, and today was the last lunch period we had to squeeze as many donations as we could from the pockets of the student body.

All the queen candidates had spent every free minute before school, during break, and all through lunch at tables in the quad, with bright, hand-colored posters announcing the club they represented and their fund-raiser. Most girls decorated their booths with ridiculous pictures of their silly project, and they tried to lure passersby and their money to their table with candy giveaways or crazy chants.

Since my fund-raiser was the only serious one in a sea of frivolity, I decided to go all the way. I created a presentation board with drunk-driving statistics. I printed out a handout with facts about spinal cord injuries and the freedom a wheelchair could provide to someone who needed one. I set up an iPad playing a rough cut of the footage Amanda had been shooting for her project, and I recruited her and Jack to help me out by talking to people who stopped by the booth to donate their spare change.

Of course, we were set up right next to Jenny Roy, who sank to new levels of ridiculous with her project of buying new Speedos for the water polo team. She even convinced some of the players, including Curt, who was earning a varsity letter in ignoring me, to actually stand at her table in their old Speedos and pass out candy with her name on it.

W. T. actual F.

"I'm sorry," Amanda said, throwing up her hands, "but she's just playing dirty. It's impossible to compete with half-naked guys with perfect bodies. I mean, who knew Rob Chang had a freaking six-pack? My God."

"Focus," I said, handing her a stack of Walk and Roll flyers. "Maybe try to get some of their overflow to sign up for our club meeting."

Crowds of students filed through the quad, stopping at the various booths and tossing change into the fund-raising jars. Our booth wasn't as busy as Naked Guy Central next door, but there were definitely students interested in Walk and Roll.

"The jar is filling up," Jack said. "Lots of pennies, though. Did you know it costs more to produce pennies than they're worth? Pennies actually cost the government money. Isn't that insane?"

"Jack," I said, rolling my eyes. "I thought we were done with the trivia."

He shoved his hands in his pockets and shrugged. "Sorry.

I'm just . . . I really want you to win, and it's making me all nervous."

I wheeled up to the table and examined my jar. It was filling up, but Jack was right. It wasn't full of dollar bills, or even quarters. People were tossing change in, but it was nothing significant. Would it be enough to actually do something meaningful with? Starting a Walk and Roll chapter was great, but winning Homecoming Queen would really get the money and attention we'd need to get some great service projects going. With a jar full of pennies, it seemed like the whole thing might fall flat.

Amanda and Jack's penny analysis, and my penny gazing, was interrupted by three girls who walked up to our booth and tossed a crumpled-up napkin covered in nacho cheese sauce into the jar.

"What the hell?" I snapped.

"You're depressing," the tallest one, clad in all black, said. "I can see why your club is called Walk and Roll. You're making me want to freaking roll myself out into traffic."

"You're the one who looks like a walking corpse," Amanda said, pulling out attitude from somewhere inside her I had no idea existed.

"Homecoming is supposed to be fun," the shortest one said. She looked a bit like a troll, and she spit when she talked. "Not a time for charity work. No one cares."

The middle one snorted. "I bet you're just raising this money for yourself. So you can buy yourself a new wheelchair or something."

I tightened my hand into a fist and held back the string of profanities that I wanted to spit at them. "Better than stealing my clothes from Goodwill."

It wasn't my best comeback ever, but they didn't listen,

anyway. They walked off, probably in search of a booth that was less depressing. But they left behind the seeds of doubt they had planted.

"What's wrong with people?" Jack grabbed my hand and squeezed it, but I yanked it away. I wasn't in the mood for comfort.

Instead, I covered my face with my hands. "They're right. This was stupid. I never should have done this."

Jack squatted down next to me and looked me right in the eyes. "You know that's not true," he said. "You're doing something good. Most people respect that. Sure, there are some A-holes, but just ignore them, okay? You're amazing."

"Look at her." I pointed to Jenny's booth, which started to resemble a beehive with all the people buzzing around it. "She's had a crowd the whole time."

"Crowds don't matter," Amanda said, leaning back against our table. "Not if she's not making any—"

"Even Alice from the Japanese Club has more people stopping at her booth than we do. She's raising money to do an anime intro on the morning announcement video. Is that more important to people than a fund-raiser that will actually help people? Our club could save lives. What do they do?"

Self-doubt was drowning me, crashing down on me like waves. I had no idea what I was doing. Thinking that anyone else besides me and my friends cared about drunk driving and spinal cord injuries was ridiculous. Those girls were right. I thought I could swoop in here with my tragic story and change the world, but really, Speedos were going to win every time.

Could I drop out of the running now? No, everyone would know I quit out of embarrassment. But I'd just be humiliated at the Homecoming assembly, when I lost after having raised hardly any money for my club.

I was seconds away from asking Jack and Amanda to help me brainstorm an exit strategy when Baker, a guy from my English class, came up to our booth and shoved a twenty-dollar bill in the jar.

"Wow." Baker had been on my radar since he spoke up in my behalf to Mr. David when I first came back to school, but this was quite a shock. No one had donated that much yet, and his generosity quickly snapped me out of my spiral of self-pity. "Thank you, Baker. Really."

"No big deal." He shoved his hands in his pockets and stared at the ground, his voice growing quiet. "My cousin Owen has been in a wheelchair for five years. He was in a drunk-driving accident, too. It killed his twin brother."

Amanda's hand flew to her mouth, and I gasped. I couldn't help it.

"I know," he said, scratching the back of his head. "It . . . it sucked. So, uh, if you need any help with Walk and Roll or anything, just let me know. I'm down to do whatever I can."

Jack walked up to Baker and slapped him on the back. "That's awesome, man. Thanks." The two of them walked behind the booth, talking about this drunk-driving awareness program called Rally4Reality that the Walk and Roll Foundation put on at Baker's cousin's high school and coming up with ideas on how Student Government could help host it.

Baker was just the reality check I needed. Jenny Roy's booth may have drawn in the quantity, but there were some people on campus who knew there were more important things in life than Speedos. I'd take that kind of quality any day.

The night before Homecoming, Amanda came over to help me get ready for the Homecoming assembly. Our school loved to make the Homecoming hoopla last as long as possible, so we held an all-school assembly during the day on Friday to crown the queen. Friday night was the Homecoming football game, where the queen got to be escorted by her dad down a red carpet on the field during halftime. Finally, the Homecoming Dance was on Saturday night, so all the girls would have plenty of time to get done up, and the queen and her date were the guests of honor. It was all a production, but it was usually pretty fun. This year, though, it was causing me nothing but stress. Good thing I had Amanda to help me get organized.

After my dress, shoes, and makeup for the assembly were all laid out and ready to go, the two of us sat on my bed, watching TV and talking about our plans for the dance. I was going with Jack, and Amanda had gotten up the nerve to ask Sergio, this guy from her media class she'd been admiring from afar, and he'd said yes. She was in the middle of dissecting their most recent text exchange with me when she jumped to her feet, excited. "I totally forgot. I have an early cut of my video project ready. You want to see?"

"Of course I do! Grab my laptop."

Amanda picked up my computer from my desk and grabbed a disk from her bag, which she slid into the side of my laptop. "You can keep this disk for now, and I'll get you a copy of the final one when it's ready to go."

As soon as she clicked Play, music blasted through the speakers as various shots of me over the past week—in my chair at school, campaigning for Homecoming, working out my legs at PT—collaged across the screen. Then my name popped up. KARA MOORE: *NOT* AN INSPIRATION.

I laughed so hard and so suddenly that I choked on it. "Awesome," I said as it followed up with, AT LEAST NOT IN THE WAY YOU THINK.

The video moved on to a series of pictures of me dancing, starting from when I was a little kid.

I smiled as the images of me in various sparkly costumes flashed across the screen, but seeing Mini Kara leaping through the air, no clue that her dancing time was so limited, sent little stabs of pain through my heart. "Where did you get these?"

"Your mom. She had a blast going through them and picking out her favorites."

Knowing Mom, she probably acted like the trip down memory lane was fun while Amanda was there, but cried her eyes out the second she was alone with all these pictures and the past. When I lost dance, she lost her role as Dance Mom, and it turns out that was just as much a part of her identity as dancing was for me.

The dance montage moved into an accident montage, causing me to gasp in shock when a photo of the crash I had never seen before filled the screen. I'd looked at the accident photos only that one night, so it made sense that there might be pictures of it I hadn't seen. I liked it that way, though. I wasn't ready to have those living in my head.

Luckily, before I had too much time to dwell on the accident photos, the video moved on, now flashing quickly from clip to clip of my new active life, with music and a voiceover from the little interviews I'd done with Amanda playing over it all. "I want my life to be full of possibilities, not regret, you know?" my voice said over a shot of me sitting on the table at PT, the tech bending and straightening my knee. Amanda also worked in captions in colorful fonts and cool transitions between the clips. And over and over it emphasized that, yes, I was in a wheelchair. But that didn't change the fact that I was a normal, active high school senior. I wasn't strong or brave or an inspiration any more than anyone who got up and came to school every day was.

I was just me.

"It looks professional," I told Amanda as she turned to me to see my reaction. "I knew you were talented at this stuff, but . . . wow."

"This is just the first version so I can turn it in to Mr. Graham for credit tomorrow. After the election, I'm going to do a longer version that has all the Homecoming results included, too, and that'll be the one I submit for the scholarship."

I beamed up at my best friend. "You're going to win for sure."

"And you're going to win Homecoming Queen for sure," she said, leaning down and hugging me.

"You know, I might not. It's just great that we raised money and have like fifteen members for Walk and Roll already."

She elbowed me playfully. "You sound like one of those 'It's an honor just to be nominated' people at the Oscars."

"Well, it's true. We're doing something good. That's what matters, right?"

"Right. But you can't tell me that Mrs. Mendoza putting that crown on your head tomorrow wouldn't feel amazing."

It would. I knew it would. But I also knew that Mr. David had been right when he told me I would never win. The school would never vote me as Homecoming Queen, not like this. So there was no point in getting my hopes up only to be disappointed.

Anyone good at making videos? Last minute!

It was the subject on the first post on my disabilities message board, and I normally would have passed right over it in favor of someone's PT update or success story, but Amanda's video was fresh on my mind, so I tapped on it out of curiosity.

The post was a link to a contest for videos about overcoming adversity, sponsored by a local news channel. They put the videos on their Web site, viewers voted for their favorites, and the winner got featured on the news and won a five-hundred-dollar cash prize.

Wow. Five hundred dollars? We could really use that money to get Walk and Roll off the ground.

The post on the message board said,

Current entries are about dogs and/or babies. I think one of you WheelFriends can totally rock this contest if you can throw together a quick video.

Yes, I thought as I read through the requirements. *Amanda's video would be perfect for this.* But there was a deadline. The contest closed tonight at midnight, only an hour away, and Amanda's video wasn't even finished yet. No time for her to get it done. No time to even really talk to her about submitting it.

And wasn't I always saying I wasn't an inspiration? Would entering myself into a contest like this make me a complete hypocrite?

It's not like her video would win, though. I mean, she did an amazing job on the technical stuff, but my story wasn't all that life-changing. Would anyone even care?

I looked at the post on the message board again. *I think one of you WheelFriends can totally rock this contest.*

Without letting myself think about it, I grabbed my laptop from the table next to my bed. I filled out the short entry form on the news station's Web site, and I uploaded Amanda's unfinished video from the disk she left in my computer. After I clicked Submit and pressed my laptop shut, I snuggled under my covers, closed my eyes, and I fell asleep easily for the first time in a month.

CHAPTER 20

It was about half an hour before the Homecoming assembly was going to start, and I'd be lying if I said that puking didn't sound like a fabulous idea. I knew I looked put together on the outside—Mom had curled my hair and given me a perfect smoky eye and glossy lip this morning, and I wore a long, spaghetti-strapped hot pink sequined dress, tight all the way down to the ankles. But inside I felt like I could fall apart at any second.

All the queen candidates and our escorts assembled in the small room adjacent to the gym, where Student Government was putting the finishing touches on their balloon arches and students were starting to file in. I was doing my best to keep my nerves under control, but unfortunately, my shaky hands were a dead giveaway to what was going on inside my head.

"Don't be nervous," Jack said, leaning over to kiss my

cheek. "You look amazing." Jack was my escort for the assembly, and he looked adorable in his black suit and hot pink tie, which matched my dress perfectly. He looked like a model in his sleek suit, and I was impressed that he even took off his beanie and tamed his mess of blond waves for the occasion.

"You like my shoes?" After some research, I did end up getting new ones—a fierce pair of ankle-strapped black patent leather five-inch stilettos that I didn't have to worry about wobbling in when I walked, wouldn't give me blisters, and stayed on nice and snug.

"I like everything about you," he said. He leaned down so his lips brushed ever-so-slightly against my ear, and he whispered, "And I'd show you just how much, if we weren't standing right in front of my math teacher."

Laughing calmed me down considerably, and for a second I managed to forget that I was about to parade myself around in front of the entire school. But reality slapped me in the face with an open hand when Jenny Roy, smug as ever in a tiny red strapless dress, strutted in with a suited-up Curt.

And they were holding hands.

I think my mouth might have fallen open at the sight of them, but I managed to close it before Jack noticed. I couldn't stop the sinking feeling in my stomach, though. I'd known Jenny was after Curt, obviously. He'd been her main mission in life before I was even in the picture, but this was a new development.

And I'd gotten over Curt. Really, I had. Losing him was a different sort of loss than my legs, a misery that lived in a different part of my heart. I'd spent a lot of time crying and wondering what I could have done differently, how I could have changed to make him love me again. But the more I thought about it, the more I realized that Curt had been really heartless. I shouldn't have to *try* to make him love me again when I'd done nothing wrong. I'd loved him and trusted him and he'd completely betrayed me when I needed him the most. He was the one who'd done something wrong, not me, and I didn't want or need someone like that in my life.

It took Jack showing me what I deserved to figure it out.

But even knowing all of that, it still stung like a swarm of angry bees to see Curt holding hands with Jenny. To see that she finally got what she wanted.

It would have been nice to avoid them, but that was impossible. Jenny headed in my direction the second she spotted me, like a heat-seeking missile of awful, and she dragged a terror-stricken Curt behind her.

"Hey, Pity Vote," she said. "Did your little club end up raising any money? Or was it just a bunch of dirty napkins in your jar?"

I was about to continue on my Kill Her with Kindness campaign, which really seemed to annoy her more than sinking to her level did, but to my surprise, I didn't have a chance. "Stop it, Jenny!" Curt snapped at her, dropping her hand. He still looked terror-stricken, but now his cheeks were pink with embarrassment, too. "Leave it alone."

She rolled her eyes. "God, I was only—"

Curt cut her off. "Kara, can I talk to you a second? Alone?"

He wanted to talk? Now? Ha, this would be good. I nodded, and looked up at Jack, who was watching the whole exchange with an expression of utter disbelief. "I'll just be a minute, okay?" I told him.

Jack glared at Curt, but he nodded anyway. "Jenny, I

think you need to check in with Mrs. Mendoza," he said. "Let's go." He reached over and grabbed Jenny's bony arm, dragging her over to Mrs. Mendoza, who was scanning her clipboard and barking out orders.

"Look, Kara," Curt said when we were Jenny-free. His eyes focused squarely on his shoes, and his voice shook. "I, um. I owe you an apology."

I was about to say, *It's okay. No big deal,* because Old Kara would have forgiven Curt anything. He could've purposely run over Logan with his truck, and I probably would have blamed my poor little dog. But I wasn't Old Kara anymore; I was Kara 2.0. So I said, "Yeah, you do."

This unexpected response from me made his head snap up, and we looked at each other, really looked at each other, for the first time since my accident. The eye contact sent a flutter through my belly, but it wasn't a flutter of attraction or wanting. It was just familiarity. Nostalgia.

And it passed as quickly as it arrived, with disgust and anger taking its place. And these emotions took root.

"You never came to see me." My blood pumped at full speed through my veins, but I managed to keep my voice even. "You never answered any of my texts. Then you were a total dick to me in front of everyone. And that's how you break up with your girlfriend of almost a year? Public humiliation? That's all I was worth to you?"

"I don't know why I said what I said." Curt had never looked so small to me. He seemed to be folding into himself, bracing himself against the truth of my words. "Or why I didn't come see you in the hospital. I just . . . I panicked, okay? I was so freaked out and I didn't know how to deal with you"—he waved his hand at my legs—"like this."

The way he said it, it was like I was somehow no longer human to him. And if I'd been wondering if any residual feelings for Curt had been lurking anywhere inside me, that casual dismissal set fire to them and blew away the ashes.

"Like *what?*"

It was obvious this was difficult for him; his face looked pinched, like it did when he was almost done with a water polo game and his muscles were about to give out on him. But I wasn't going to go easy on him. He owed me more than an apology; he owed me the truth, and I wanted to hear him say what he thought of me. Damaged. Broken.

"Hurt," he said, his voice breaking. "I didn't know how to handle seeing you so hurt. If we hadn't fought, you wouldn't have been in the car. I felt so guilty, and I was scared, so I freaked out and I hid. It was the totally wrong thing to do, and I am so, so sorry, Kara. I know you'll probably never forgive me, and I don't blame you. But I just had to—"

"If it had been you in the accident, Curt, I would have been there every day in the hospital. I would've never left your side."

He covered his face with his shaky hands. "I know."

How could I have spent so much time with him? How could I have thought he cared about me? How could I have cared about him?

"Well, thanks for your apology," I said. "I appreciate it." I wasn't ready to forgive him yet, but I was definitely ready for this conversation to be over.

Curt took a deep breath, and it seemed to pull him back together. "So, you're back with Jack, huh?" He let out a small, humorless laugh. "I should have seen that one coming."

While I wanted to tell Curt how happy I was with Jack,

how I finally felt like myself with him, something I never felt with Curt, and how Jack never forgot to pick me up, no matter how busy he was, I didn't. He didn't get to know that about me. He didn't get to know anything about me anymore. So I just said, "Yeah." Then, because I had to, "So, you and Jenny?"

He shrugged.

"Well, good luck to you guys." I wanted to add that he was going to need it to deal with her, but I felt like the bigger person here, so I kept that one to myself. "I better go find Jack."

And I turned my wheelchair around as quickly as I could, away from Curt, finally mastering that dramatic exit.

CHAPTER 21

I don't know who decided to make these school assemblies so freaking long, but I wanted to find them and run their feet over with my chair. Cheerleaders cheering, class competition, drum line performance, introduction of the fall sports teams— it was all fun and games when you were sitting in the bleachers and the whole production was getting you out of second period, but it was torture to sit through when you were the very last thing on the agenda.

"Oh my God," I whispered to Jack. "Are they going to let each individual student get up and walk across the gym floor before they finally get this over with? I'm freaking out over here."

We were lined up in alphabetical order, all the queen candidates with their escorts next to them, sitting in folding chairs up against the back wall of the gym. Well, I wasn't in alphabetical order. I was stuck on the end after Maya

Zelinski. And I wasn't in a folding chair, either. But at least Jack was next to me, thank God. There's no way I could get through this without him.

"Take a deep breath," Jack said as he massaged my neck. "Did you know that changing your breathing can change your mood? In through your nose, out through your mouth, and you'll feel better in a minute or two."

If he was throwing out a fun fact at this point, he must have been as jittery as I was. But I was willing to try anything to calm myself down, so I was about to break into some yoga breathing when it was finally time to go. Mrs. Mendoza flapped her hands at us, some of Jack's friends from Student Government got on the mic to do introductions, and before I even had a chance to take a deep breath, we were all heading over to the red carpet that stretched down the middle of the gym floor.

Each candidate was called one at a time, along with her club and fund-raiser. Everyone cheered as each of the girls walked across the gym and stood against the backdrop set up at the opposite end. I have to admit, I had to hold in a laugh when Jenny wobbled on her stilettos. Petty? Probably. But it still felt pretty good.

"And last but not least," Paul, Jack's Student Government friend, said into the mic, "we have Kara Moore representing the brand-new Walk and Roll Foundation. Kara's fund-raiser was drunk- and distracted-driving awareness, and she's being escorted today by Jack Matthews."

All the other couples walked with the girl's arm slipped delicately through the guy's, looking stiff and formal. But when Jack and I made our way down the red carpet, I grabbed his hand and laced our fingers together, squeezing tight. Forcing a smile on my face, I pushed myself down the red carpet with my free hand. It wasn't easy; pushing myself down the gym floor would have been much less work one-handed than this dumb carpet. But I wanted to do this. Go down the red carpet. Hold Jack's hand. All with my head up and a smile on my face.

"Your hand is shaking," Jack whispered out the side of his mouth. "Breathe."

So I did.

Keeping my focus on Jack's steady hand wrapped around mine, I took a chance and looked out into the bleachers, which were full of students packed in like sardines. Most of them were talking to one another and not really paying attention, a bunch smiled and clapped, which helped me relax, and a few looked bored. Who could blame them, though? I'd probably be bored if I were them.

But there in the front, crouched down on the gym floor with her camera running and braids falling on either side of her face like a curtain, was Amanda. I knew she would be filming the assembly; she said she wanted to add footage from Homecoming into the final version of the project before she submitted it for the scholarship. I didn't think I would be able to find her in the crowd, though. I smiled into the small lens of her camera, and she lifted her free hand and gave me a thumbs-up. Her support, and the pressure of Jack's fingers on mine, buoyed me, and I made it to the end of the red carpet without puking into my own lap.

Once Jack and I were in place, in the center of the line of candidates and escorts, the Student Government students handed Mrs. Mendoza a mic, and I knew it was time to go. I tuned her out as she thanked the student body for their participation in Homecoming by donating and voting, and I focused on squeezing Jack's hand until she finally looked at our line and smiled.

"I'm pleased to announce that this year's Homecoming Queen is . . ."

Jack squeezed my hand again. I squeezed back so hard, I thought I might crush his fingers.

I held my breath.

"Jenny Roy, whose fund-raising project raised enough money for two new sets of game uniforms for the varsity and junior varsity water polo teams!"

Alice from the Japanese Club, who was standing next to me, snorted quietly. "Game uniforms. Right."

Somehow, through the whole assembly, I'd kept a smile plastered on my face. But as soon as Jenny's name was announced, my stomach dropped to the floor, disappointment flooded through my system, and I had no idea if that smile was still there or not.

I lost.

I lost and Jenny Roy won.

This wasn't how it was supposed to go. After everything I'd lost already—Curt, dancing, my legs—it was my turn to win. That's how it was supposed to happen. That's how karma was supposed to work.

But in my heart, I'd always known I wouldn't ever be Homecoming Queen. Even way back when Curt told me I was his nominee, back before my accident, before the wheelchair. I never let myself really want it, because I knew deep inside I would never actually get it. Girls like Jenny, who thrust themselves into the spotlight and thrived on attention, were Homecoming material. They were always the girls who won.

So I wasn't surprised. Or disappointed. I really wasn't.

But.

I wanted to prove to everyone that I could. I let myself want it.

Why had I been so stupid?

The students who were packed into the gym all screamed and cheered, and Mrs. Mendoza placed a sparkly plastic tiara on Jenny's head, while Jenny smiled her fake smile and tried to look sincerely surprised. She jumped up and down and hugged Curt and bent her head so Mrs. Mendoza could wrap a sash around her shoulder that said HOMECOMING QUEEN.

Jenny, who would get to walk across the field during half-time at tonight's football game with her dad. Jenny, who would get to dance with Curt in a spotlight tomorrow night at the dance. Jenny, who, over and over, kept getting the things I wanted.

I plastered a smile back on my face and clapped politely for her. So did Jack. I wondered if my sadness and disappointment were over the fact that I didn't pull it off or the fact that Jenny did. I wondered if I'd be this conflicted to see Mrs. Mendoza crowning Alice or Maya Zelinski or one of the other girls Homecoming Queen right now.

All the queen candidates and escorts followed Jenny and Curt back down the red carpet and filed into the backstage room, and I couldn't wheel myself back down the red carpet fast enough. I was sick of this attention. I wanted to go back to trying to fly under the radar.

Jack waved me over to a quiet corner of the room, and he kneeled down in front of me, gripping the handles of my chair. "It doesn't matter, you know." He trailed the tips of his fingers lightly up and down my arm as he spoke, making goose bumps sprout up on my skin. "The crown and the

sash don't matter. You raised money for something that matters. You started something important here. That's so much
more than she can say."

A long sigh escaped my lips. "I know. You're right." And
he was. "But I'm still bummed, you know?"

I looked up and noticed that a strange crowd of people
waited in the room, probably to shower attention on Jenny
Roy and her stupid tiara. At least if she was distracted by a
crowd of adoring fans, I could slip away, change, and get myself back to class unnoticed. A smug comment from her was
the last thing I needed right now.

"Hurry," I said to Jack. "Grab your stuff and let's sneak out
of here. Can I change in the activities office? I need to get out of
this dress. The straps are digging into my shoulders like crazy."

"Do you need help?" Jack said with a smile. "Because I'm
pretty useful at those sorts of tasks."

But we didn't get a chance to make a quick exit, because
the strange people didn't crowd around Jenny; they pushed
right past her, actually. Who were they?

"Kara! Kara Moore! Can we talk to you for a second?"

"What?" *Did they say my name? Why?* I turned my head
to see if someone was standing behind me, but there was nothing but the door to the gym. I turned my head up to Jack to
see if this was some kind of surprise from him, but he looked
just as confused as I felt.

"No idea," he said, shrugging.

The first woman who reached me looked vaguely familiar, but I couldn't place her. She was wearing a bright green
skirt suit and had department store–perfect makeup and a
hair helmet, and I couldn't think of why I would know anyone who dressed like that.

"Kara!" She shoved her hand into my personal space. I assumed she wanted me to shake it, so I did. She strangled my fingers and practically ripped my arm out of the socket. "So great to meet you! Do you have a second to talk to KDAK?"

"Oh," I said. "You must be confused. You want Jenny Roy. She's right over there." I pointed across the room to Jenny, who was holding up her compact and arranging her hair around the tiara, although I wasn't sure how this woman could possibly get me and Jenny confused. "I didn't know that Homecoming Queen was all that newsworthy."

The woman threw her head back and laughed, but strangely, her hair didn't move. "Oh, I'm sorry! I don't want her. I'm Dierdre Duncan from KDAK, and I'm here to talk to you about your video!"

"What?"

"We love what you're doing here at your school! And your story is so compelling! Vinny! Get over here!" She snapped her fingers at a tall, skinny guy with long dreadlocks who was holding a camera that looked to be about twice his body weight and about a zillion times more ginormous and fancy than Amanda's camera. Vinny snapped to attention at the sound of her voice, since he looked as if he'd been distracted by Jenny's primping. Or her tiny strapless dress. It took only two strides of his long, toothpick legs, and he was right by Dierdre Duncan's side, camera positioned on his shoulder.

Jack crouched down next to me. "What did you do?" he whispered.

"I'm sorry," I said, turning back to the overcaffeinated Dierdre Duncan and her hair helmet. "I have no idea what's happening."

"The video! Of everything you've done on your campus!

Starting a chapter of the Walk and Roll Foundation! Raising money! Your story has touched so many people!"

Oh my God, the video. In all the drama of Homecoming, I'd completely forgotten about my late-night upload of Amanda's video project to the news station's contest. But why would I even think about it? The videos weren't even supposed to be live until the weekend.

"We pushed it live on the site this morning and featured it on the home page! You have thousands of views already! Thousands!" She ran her tongue over her teeth. "Okay, Vinny! Let's do this!" She pulled out a microphone with the KDAK logo on the side and dropped her bag on the floor with a thud.

And just liked that, Vinny was rolling, Dierdre Duncan counted down, and I stared at the red light on Vinny's camera like I'd been smacked in the face with a frying pan.

"I'm Dierdre Duncan, here at Pacific Coastal High School, with seventeen-year-old Homecoming Queen finalist Kara Moore, whose inspiring YouTube video chronicling her journey to recovery after a drunk-driving accident left her paralyzed from the waist down has become an overnight sensation." Dierdre Duncan's professional television voice was a little deeper and lot less enthusiastic than her conversation voice, and the disparity only added to this completely surreal experience.

"Kara, tell us a little bit about the video." She shoved the mic in my face.

"Well, uh, the video is actually a project by my best friend, Amanda Kenyon, who created it for a scholarship contest. It's not even done yet, really, and—"

"What was the topic of the contest? And why did Amanda choose you as her subject?"

I smoothed my hands, which were becoming sweatier and sweatier with every second that passed, down the lap of my sequined dress. "The topic was active teens, and Amanda thought it would be cool to show that it was possible to be active even in a wheelchair, to show that kids with disabilities can do more than people think. If you want to talk to her about it, I can—"

"Well, you've certainly proved that, Kara. Now, the beginning of the video states that you're not an inspiration in the way we expect. What do you mean by that?"

"People do amazing things all the time. I did the best I could with the things that happened in my life, just the way anyone else would. I don't think that's particularly inspirational, it's just my reality. I'm not trying to inspire anyone, I'm just trying to be myself."

A crowd had formed behind Vinny. Queen candidates, escorts, Student Government officers, teachers, even Jenny and Curt stood by, heads cocked to the side, and watched Dierdre interview me. All eyes were on me, but for once, I didn't feel analyzed and judged. For the first time in so long, I was flooded with that familiar euphoria from performing for an audience that I hadn't felt since the last time I danced.

I was talking about something that mattered, and people were listening.

"Kara, can you tell us why you decided to forgo the silly fund-raisers that are so popular with the other Homecoming candidates here on campus in favor of drunk-driving awareness?"

"I guess I saw the opportunity to do something productive and I took it." The more I spoke, the more my confidence built, like a ladder that I could climb up. My words came out stronger, louder. Having an attentive audience helped, too. Maybe it was just because of the cameras, but I felt like everyone was really listening to me for the first time since the accident. "If I'm going to raise money for a cause, I want it to be for something that matters. People on the campus need to be aware of the dangers of drunk and distracted driving. As teenagers, we seem to think that bad things can't happen to us, but I'm proof that they can, so I want to equip the students here with ways to keep it from happening again."

"That's fantastic, Kara. Pacific Coastal High is lucky to have such a hardworking and motivated student on this campus. Now, Kara, we actually have a surprise for you."

And from behind Dierdre Duncan, a short, balding man in a red polo shirt whom I hadn't noticed stepped toward me holding a huge piece of paper.

"Kara, this is Mr. Sam Taylor, the owner of Taylor's Tires."

I smiled at him, not entirely sure what some tire guy had to do with any of this.

Mr. Taylor smiled back, and cleared his throat. "Kara, I was so moved by your video. My wife was involved in a car accident about fifteen years ago now, and she also suffered a spinal cord injury and has been in a wheelchair ever since." His voice broke, but he kept talking. "I think it's great what you're doing here at your school, and I wanted to make a donation to your club on behalf of Taylor's Tires."

He lifted the big piece of paper he was holding, which turned out to be one of those huge checks. A huge check for one thousand dollars, made out to the Walk and Roll Foundation.

One thousand dollars.

What was my life right now? Who, in real life, actually got a giant check? No one. That wasn't a real thing that happened to real people. Especially giant checks from strangers, who handed you huge donations out of the blue.

But nothing that had happened to me in the past few months felt like a real thing that happened to real people. Maybe once you went through some crazy stuff, the universe rewarded you with things that were more amazing than you could have ever imagined. I mean, I'd entered the video contest on a whim, thinking the club could really use five hundred dollars. Now the contest hadn't even started, and we were being handed twice that because I'd put myself out there and shared my story.

Dierdre shifted back in front of Mr. Taylor. "In fact, we've had viewers contacting the station all morning, Kara, asking us how to get in touch with you to donate to your cause." She turned and faced Vinny and the camera directly. "Viewers, if you've been moved by Kara's story and would like to donate to the Pacific Coastal High School's chapter of the Walk and Roll Foundation and Kara's campaign to increase drunk- and distracted-driving awareness among local teens, please visit the link on your screen."

Dierdre Duncan wrapped up her broadcast, but I was too stunned to pay attention. Not only did I have this big check for a thousand freaking dollars handed to me by a man I'd never met, but I now had random people who watched the news calling in and demanding to know where they could find me to give me money. Unbelievable.

I found Jack's face in the crowd. He was standing next to Amanda, who was getting all this on camera, and he was beaming at me. "What is happening?" I mouthed across the sea of people who had gathered.

He laughed. "Just go with it," he mouthed back.

Dierdre Duncan thanked me and shook my hand, and before I could register what was happening, the crowd descended upon me. Person after person, student, teacher, random I'd never seen before, all in my face, telling me how awesome this all was, asking to join Walk and Roll, and telling me how excited they were for everything I was doing.

Finally, I was face-to-face with Mr. Taylor. He ran his hand over his balding head.

"Thanks for everything, Kara." Mr. Taylor stuck out his hand, and I shook it. "My wife was a dancer, too, before her accident. Seeing your video really made her smile. You truly are an inspiration."

And the way he said it didn't make me bristle. It didn't make me feel like I was some Other that every able-bodied person was tossing pity toward.

I felt like I really was doing something positive. Like I really was inspiring people. Not through what I was no longer able to do, but because of what I was doing now.

Maybe I was an inspiration after all. Not because I managed to get up and show my face in public every day in a wheelchair, making everyone else feel better about their lives, but because I was taking my experiences and using them to make things better for other people. I wasn't going to let this bad thing that happened define me, and I had no intention of ever giving up on the things I wanted.

If that was what it meant to be an inspiration, I was totally okay with that.

CHAPTER 22

I'd missed driving. It always calmed me down and cleared my head, and just pushing myself really fast in my wheelchair never seemed to have the same effect.

Not like this.

Today, with the window rolled down, the rush of fresh air blew my hair in whips across my face. It was sunny and clear, though, one of those perfect California winter days in early December, and the sun warmed the skin on my arm through the open car window.

The road stretched out in front of me, and I was behind the wheel again. I felt free.

I was on my way to pick up Jack and Amanda, so I could take them out for a drive for a change. But I took the long way to their neighborhood, remembering the feeling of driving, how it made me calm, centered me, and helped me think.

Right after Homecoming, Mom got a part-time job at the dance studio, replacing Susan the receptionist, who spent more time at Starbucks than behind the front desk anyway. Mom loved her new job, where she felt like she was part of something, and where she was free to Dance Mom as much as she wanted to all over the girls there. Plus, Mom working even a few days a week was doing wonders for my parents' relationship. The fighting hadn't ended, it probably never would, but they were going to marriage counseling weekly, stopping their fights in the middle and reminding each other of whatever psychobabble their therapist Dr. Patel had gone over with them the week before, and Logan wasn't hiding under my bed nearly so much as he used to.

One thing my parents didn't fight about at all was Mom truly surprising me by using some of her new income from the studio to supplement the insurance money from the accident and help buy me a new car. She threw herself into finding the perfect car for me, and she scoured the Internet to find me a car equipped with hand controls for paraplegic drivers and finally settled on a small SUV. It looked like a normal car, even though it wasn't anywhere near as cute as my Prius was, but I was able to accelerate and brake from a lever I squeezed with my hand. I could drive without using my legs at all.

Sure, I had to learn how to drive it, which was like having my learner's permit all over again, and it was super bizarre and counterintuitive at first, using my hands instead of my feet. But since I couldn't feel my feet anyway, I didn't have the same impulses to hit the brakes as I once did. And, yeah, I had to take the dumb test all over in my new car, but it was worth it to be back on the road again.

I honked as I pulled up in Jack's driveway, but Jack and Amanda must have been waiting for me, because they rushed out the front door before I'd even moved my hand off the horn. They swung the doors to my car open, and Jack sat next to me in the front while Amanda crawled into the backseat, next to my folded-up wheelchair.

"How does it feel?" Jack asked after kissing me hello.

Smiling, I backed out of the driveway and turned onto the street. "Even better than I remember."

"So, where are we heading?" Amanda leaned back in the backseat. The wind from the open windows blew her braids into her face from all sides.

"I have no idea," I said. "I'm open to suggestions. The world is our oyster."

Jack leaned across the center console and whispered in my ear. "I don't care what we do, as long as we can ditch Amanda later. I love her and all, but I have some plans that involve getting you alone."

Heat rushed to my cheeks, setting my face on fire. Jack never stopped talking to me or about me like I belonged on the pages of *Maxim*, and I'm not gonna lie, I absolutely loved it.

"You do wonders for my ego," I said, smiling.

"Well, you do wonders for my—"

"So, when are we going to plan that Walk and Roll movie night we've been talking about?" Amanda broke in from the backseat. "Baker has been really excited about getting this new programming off the ground. How about next Friday?"

"Can't," I said, trying to focus on the conversation instead of Jack's hand burning a hole through my shoulder. "Mom and I are driving up the coast to visit colleges next weekend, and we have a lot of research to do to make up for lost time. We want to check out all the schools I applied to."

"Okay, fine," Amanda said, looking at the calendar on her phone. "What about the weekend after that?"

"That's my first performance! And you said you'd come watch me dance, remember?"

After the video went viral, I started talking pretty frequently to Mr. Taylor's wife, Lorin. It turned out Lorin was active in the local wheelchair community, which I didn't even realize was a thing outside of the Internet. Lurking on my message boards was awesome, but once I started doing some research, I was amazed at how wonderful it felt to be surrounded with people in real life going through the same things as I was.

A night out to dinner with Lorin led to my most amazing discovery ever—a local wheelchair dance team: a group of both dancers in wheelchairs and able-bodied dancers who performed at schools and expos and conventions across the state. Mom and I spent hours that night watching videos of all their performances online, surprised and thrilled to find out that they were actually really talented dancers. The next morning I'd arranged to meet with them for an audition, and a week later I was rehearsing with the team and talking about teaming up with Walk and Roll. Adding a dance team to the Walk and Roll programming was going to make our foundation that much more awesome.

And I was dancing again. Even in a wheelchair, I was dancing.

"I wouldn't miss it for the world," Amanda said. "But you'll need to figure out some time in your calendar for the movie night, Miss Popular. You have so much going on."

She was right. Only a few months after my accident, after losing the use of my legs and thinking my life was over, my calendar was already packed again with the things I loved. Dancing. Driving. Friends. It didn't always seem like it would, but life had a way of coming together in ways I couldn't even anticipate. So, maybe walking again wouldn't be so impossible for me after all. But even if I never walked again, I was absolutely confident that my future was full of possibilities that I couldn't even imagine.

"We'll figure something out," I said to her, smiling at the open road ahead of me. "Everything works out the way it's supposed to."